Eleven-year-old Mike and his family were moving from the city of Wichita to a small Colorado town. But Mike did not want to go. It meant leaving all his friends, his paper route, his second-base spot on the Little League team. When they got to Colorado, and Mike found that it was cold, and that the people were strange and unfriendly, he decided to run away home — back to Wichita.

How Mike earns money for his secret trip and how he wins an honored place in the heart of his new community is the heart of this sensitive story.

ALFRED A. KNOPF  NEW YORK

Run Away Home

Mary Francis Shura

ILLUSTRATED BY JAMES SPANFELLER

L.C. Catalog card number: 65-11968

This is a Borzoi Book, published by Alfred A. Knopf, Inc.

Copyright © 1965 by Mary Francis Shura.

 TO MIMI

WHO MADE HOME NOT A PLACE,

BUT A BELONGING

Contents

Run Away Home

1

THE FOLDED APRON

It was just like any other hot July afternoon, any other Wednesday afternoon that is, until Dad came home. Mike had collected from his paper route customers and was sitting on the kitchen floor sorting the money into neat piles of nickels, dimes, and quarters. Five-year-old Elsie was squatting beside him, watching wide-eyed and helping him. Anyway, she thought she was helping.

Mike would just have a number straight in his head when Elsie would say firmly, "Fourteen, seventeen, tenteen, eighteen." Then Mike would have to start all over again.

"There's Daddy," Mike told her invitingly as he heard sounds on the back porch. He sighed with contentment as she squealed off. He was completely absorbed in his counting when a sudden stillness in the room made him look up.

His older sister Merrie stood stock still where she was setting the table, her hand holding a plate in mid-air. Elsie was now in Dad's arms with her blond head tight against his chest and her legs wound around his waist to hold on.

Dad was looking at Mom. Mike saw something different pass between them in that look, something too different to understand.

As if it were a signal, slowly and carefully, without saying a word, Mom reached behind her and unfastened the ties of her blue plaid apron. As if she were sleepwalking, she folded the apron carefully and laid it in the drawer.

When she turned back to Dad she was smiling, and the quick lilt of her voice was just like always. "All right, hands clean everybody. Supper's ready and Daddy's hungry."

Maybe Mike just imagined that Dad kissed Mom more tenderly than usual as he passed the stove with

Elsie still hanging on tight. Mike was certain that Mom gave Dad an extra hug. Mike looked at Merrie but found no help there. She was finishing the table, folding napkins by the plates with a strange, faraway look in her eyes.

Mike stared at Merrie, wishing fiercely that he could catch her attention. Grudgingly, Mike admitted that Merrie was pretty. A fellow shouldn't really admit things like that about a sister, even if she was seventeen and practically a grownup. He would certainly never admit it out loud. But Merrie really was pretty, with soft brown hair and a strange kind of gray eyes that had a way of saying a lot. What her eyes said, as she turned to look at him now, was plain. "It'll be fine," she was telling him. "So what'll be fine?" he wondered. Just then Elsie whirled by and scrambled into her chair. Mike knew that he would know when he was told and that was that.

Usually there was a little quick discussion about who would say the blessing, but tonight Merrie spoke up quickly. "I think it's my turn," she said quietly. Dad looked at her questioningly as she finished the Wayfarer's grace, but he said nothing.

"What's new in anybody's world?" Dad asked, deftly separating Elsie's pork chop from its bone, then just as neatly separating the bone from Elsie's quick fingers.

"Gravy in there," Elsie ordered, pointing to a lop-sided excavation she had made in her potatoes.

"The Majestic Laundry team is in second place," Mike said calmly.

"That's where they were last week," Mom laughed. "That's no news."

"That's the kind of no news that's good news." Mike grinned. "I like to talk about it. We could get beaten, you know. It isn't likely," he said, "but it's possible."

"I think that's great, son," Dad agreed. "And I'm sure they owe it all to their second baseman!"

The combination of crisp pork chops and fragrant apple rings kept Mike too busy to wonder any more about that strange, quiet moment of Dad's home-coming. After supper, he raced out to baseball practice.

Almost before he could believe it, the sun was near setting, and the fellows were being whistled home.

Mike watched the contrail of a jet plane swinging a wide curve towards Oklahoma. The stream was scarlet from the setting sun, and the sky was filled with strands of color that were almost as bright in the east as the west.

Right here, inside Wichita, it wasn't any problem to

remember what century you lived in, but just north of town, where the prairie sky gleamed brightly, the long stretch of the Flint Hills began. Even along the wide concrete of the turnpike, Mike would never have been surprised to see a band of Indians rise suddenly from behind the shadowed slopes, pursuing the great herds of buffaloes that once grazed these grassy hills.

Because he had walked home so slowly, the back yard was almost dark. Mike nearly stumbled over Merrie who was hunched with her chin on her knees on the back steps. She didn't look unhappy, just thoughtful, as she stared off past the dried bunches of lilac blossoms on the bush by the steps.

"Something wrong, Sis?" he asked gently, flopping on the steps beside her, shivering from the sudden cooling of his T-shirt.

Unexpectedly, Mike felt Merrie's hand on his knee, and he flushed in the dark. "Not really, I guess," she said slowly, "it's just something to get used to."

"Gee whiz, Merrie!" Mike exploded unhappily, "something's up, and you and Dad and Mom all look so mysterious. Can't you let a fellow in on it?"

Merrie turned to stare at him in surprise. "Didn't you

see Mom?" she asked, amazed. "Folding her apron and all that?"

"So she folded her apron," Mike said sarcastically. "Just as if she usually throws it on the floor or something."

"Don't be like that," Merrie said firmly. "Just think about it. Did you ever see Mom put her apron away like that . . . dirty, and with dinner and dishes not through? Didn't you see the way she kind of froze and then gave Dad that funny little sleepwalking smile?"

"It was funny, all right," Mike agreed. "What did it mean?"

"It means that all the talk around town is true. It means that the plant didn't get the contract. Mike, this is an aircraft town. Dad was transferred here from Oregon because of that. With the plant cutting down. . . ." Her voice trailed off, and Mike waited.

"It means we'll move again," she said flatly, in a careful kind of voice.

"Move," he squealed. "Move where?"

Merrie shrugged. "Who knows."

"But this is HOME!" Mike protested.

Merrie nodded. "I know. It's always hard, but well

. . . the new place gets to be home and is just as hard to leave. It's funny."

"I can't really remember any place before this," Mike said thoughtfully.

"Surely you remember when Mom and Dad bought this house, when Elsie was born," Merrie protested with surprise.

"I can remember the moving van, and something about a sand pile, but I can't picture that other house in my mind at all. When I think about it, it seems like this one . . . the furniture and everything."

Merrie nodded. "It was the same furniture. I can remember when we moved into that one." She smiled at him in the dark. "We rented it unfurnished and it was really hollow sounding for awhile. We needed the bigger house because you were born, and nobody wanted to sleep with a howling Mike in their room." She thumped his knee kiddingly.

"I really cried," Merrie admitted after a minute. "I guess I was about seven. We had lived in a small apartment and the new house seemed big and scary to me."

"Apartment." Mike shook his head. "That sure doesn't sound like our family." He glanced around the darkened yard with its big trees and Elsie's tricycle tip-tilted on the slab of brick where they kept the picnic table.

Merrie shrugged. "You have to remember that it was only Mom and Dad and me. We moved to the apartment when we came from Oregon. It seemed silly to buy a house until we found out whether we liked Kansas or not."

"That must have been pretty bad," Mike said thoughtfully.

"I missed the beach mostly," Merrie admitted. "Little tiny kids don't really care where they live if they have the things they like. Mom and Dad had a sand pile put in the apartment house playground and then I was fine. Elsie will be like that, I guess."

"No wonder you knew right away that something was going on. How does that apron business work?"

Merrie grinned. "I think it is just something that Mom does instead of fussing or crying. It seems as if the moment she knows she is going to move, she starts getting it done inside her head. She does absent-minded things, as if she were sleepwalking. I can remember that even from the move from the apartment. To me, it's just a part of moving."

Moving. The word stuck painfully in Mike's mind, like a bite of apple in his throat. He searched Merrie's face in the half light. He was wrong. It was not like a bite of apple in his throat, it was as if his whole world had been caught in a painful sob. It was the paper route he had waited his turn to get and had only been working on for four months. It was the patrol in the Boy Scout troop that he was leader of. It was the second base spot on the Majestic Laundry team.

"I won't go," he said finally. "I just won't go."

Merrie sighed. Suddenly her tone was very light. She slapped his knee hard as she rose. "You'll go, old fellow, and later on, you'll be glad." She leaned over and whispered. "Just don't let Mom and Dad know how rough it is, huh? Let's just see if we can't keep it between ourselves."

Mike watched her go thoughtfully. "Between ourselves," she had said. Did that mean it would be hard for her? It couldn't, not really. After all, Merrie had just graduated from high school. She would be going to college in the fall anyway. What did it matter to her where the family lived? She had been accepted at the University of Wichita, so she would get to stay here.

Because Merrie was generally right about things, Mike kept very quiet when Dad made the formal announcement. "I'm really lucky to have located another position right away," he told them brightly, "and none of us has ever lived in Colorado. It will be a new thing, and fun."

"Does they have sandboxes in Colorado?" Elsie asked worriedly.

"Do they," Mom corrected automatically.

"If they don't, we'll introduce them." Dad winked at her. "But they have mountains and pine trees and trout streams and skiing," Dad went on convincingly. "And you have all of August to get acquainted before school begins."

"All of August," Mike thought miserably, "while someone plays second base in my place."

Later, it seemed to Mike that it had been like hitting an unexpected stretch of ice and losing his balance.

Once Mom folded her apron, it was all over for him. The house became a confusion of packing boxes and general disorder.

There was a big, ugly FOR SALE sign planted in the front yard. Strange people sent by the real estate companies called at odd hours.

Mike didn't like any of the couples who came to look at their house. They didn't seem to understand about houses. They poked around the plumbing, banged at the furnace, and studied the roof. The way they looked at the house made him feel like taking a poke at them.

"I'm glad *they* didn't want it," he told his dad after one couple left. "They wouldn't appreciate it."

Dad patted his shoulder absently. "At this point, I'd sell it to a mongoose for the right price," he said glumly. "It looks as if it isn't going to sell at all."

"That's silly, Dad," Mike protested. "It's a swell house and close to school, and look what good neighbors we have."

"It's all part of a bigger thing, Mike," Dad told him. "When the plant starts booming again, houses will sell for what they are worth. This one will, too. Then we can pick out a house that is just what we want in Colorado."

Mike hadn't thought of that. Of course, they would have to sell this house to buy one in the new town.

"But what will we do there now?" Mike asked.

"Goodness, Mike," Dad smiled at him, "we've only owned this house since Elsie was born. Before that we rented a house, and before that an apartment. There's more than one way to put a roof over your head."

"I guess I don't remember very well," Mike admitted.

"I do," Elsie said smugly.

Dad laughed. "You weren't even born, little miss. But Merrie remembers, don't you?"

She nodded. "Clear back to the beach we went to when we lived in Portland," she added.

"Of course, you can't just snap your fingers and make the perfect house appear," Dad admitted. "They tell me that property is very costly near the plant and that rental places are hard to find. Your mother and I are planning to make a quick trip out to Colorado and look around. Maybe we'll be lucky."

The trip was not as quick as Mom and Dad had planned. They were expected back on Monday, but it was Wednesday before they finally returned.

"Tell us about the new house," Merrie said excitedly before they even set the suitcase down. "How many bedrooms does it have?"

"Only three," Dad admitted regretfully. "You'll have to share with Elsie when you are home."

Mike felt suddenly shocked. That's right. Merrie wouldn't be home very much any more.

She was already enrolled in the University of Wichita.

There would be only a little time for her to live in the new house before she would be off with the new luggage she had gotten for graduation. All of them must have thought at the same time of how different this year would be . . . in a new place and with Merrie away from home. The awkward moment of silence was finally broken as Dad wrinkled his face in a puzzled expression. "You tell them," he finally said to Mom. "I don't know how to."

"Well," Mom began determinedly, "it's as different from this house as a house can be. It's not in a town at all, but out on the edge of a little village up the mountainside above Denver. It's an old house, two stories and an attic, and it sits against the prettiest cliff at the base of a mountain." She hesitated. "It's different, but lovely."

"We had to rent it furnished," Dad added. "Which is really all right because that means that we might be able to move our furniture only once . . . when this house is sold."

"But what about our things?" Merrie almost wailed.

"We'll put them into storage," Mom explained quietly. "Unless we have to rent our own house furnished. That would make it more complicated. We'll just have to wait and see."

"About the town," Mike asked confusedly. "You say there's no town at all?"

"Not much," Dad agreed. "Goldstream is really just one street of businesses with a scattering of houses and a school. It used to be a silver mining town, I understand, but now the nearest thing to an industry is a lumber company."

"The only real disadvantage," Mom said regretfully, "is that the house is quite a long drive from Daddy's plant. He won't have much time at home evenings."

"Oh, but those weekends!" Dad said gaily.

Mom laughed. "He took one glance at those clear blue streams that run through the mountains and decided that he is going to turn into a trout fisherman."

"You'll like it, too, Mike." Dad said earnestly. "It couldn't be more different from Wichita, but . . . it's just great. You'll see."

Mike tried to look convinced. Leaving Wichita was harder to imagine every day. Keeping his feelings about the move to himself was a day-to-day problem, too.

Only once did he come dangerously close to blurting out his feeling of rebellion. It was the middle of July, and their last full day at home. When all their efforts to sell the house had failed, Dad had finally rented it on a year's lease. Most of their own furniture was already in storage and the basement was filled with boxes of things that the new tenants had brought over, a car-load at a time. Dad was due at his new job the first of August. He felt the sooner they moved in and got settled, the better it would be.

"The more fishing you'll get done!" Mom teased him.

He only grinned and didn't deny it.

Mike had gone to tell some of his friends good-by. As Mike ran through the yard, he found his mother down on her knees by the lilac bush digging earnestly at the roots with a trowel.

"What are you trying to do, Mom?" he asked. "That thing is too big to move."

She grinned up at him, pushing her hair back with her garden glove. The glove left a rakish patch of mud by her eyes.

"Mike, my friend, I planted this lilac the spring we moved here." Her voice was kind of dreamy. "We've planted a lilac from this same start in every back yard we've ever had."

"Even the rented places where you only stayed a little while?" Mike asked, surprised.

She nodded. "Home is home," she said almost stubbornly. "And it's fun in the spring to think about all of the lilacs blooming at all those back doors." Mike took the trowel and began to dig about the roots of the little shoot she had been attacking.

"Sort of a Johnny Lilac Seed, aren't you?" he teased. "Let me help with the Colorado donation."

"As much as I hate to admit it, Mike," she said and smiled, watching him rock the little plant loose with a bundle of earth still tight about its roots, "you are a pretty good boy."

He grinned back at her. "And your garden gloves don't match, either."

Because the trip to Goldstream would take two long days, Dad got them up very early to start. With the last of their things tucked into the little rented trailer, they pulled quietly out of their driveway just as the sun came up.

Mike watched the familiar places pass with a sinking heart. Even after they reached the open country, he could look back at the skyline of Wichita and identify some places. There was the tall shaft of the downtown hotel where he and Mom always went for chocolate sodas because their cafe made the best, absolutely the very best, sodas in all Kansas. He watched a small plane circling to land out south where wide, green fields surrounded low hangars, and trim lines of planes poised eagerly like runners awaiting a starting signal.

The first day's travel took them through oil fields where the well pumps worked the earth like little metal woodpeckers, past wheat fields freshly harvested, and wide stretches of buffalo grass brightened by herds of red-and-white cattle.

By the second day, even Merrie was cross. She insisted that Mike's shepherd dog, Buckshot, was breathing on her all the time. Elsie whimpered with tiredness and homesickness. And Mike felt as if the constant wind which he had always loved before, was blowing away his world as they drove west.

Then they were in the mountains. From Denver to Goldstream, the road wound and wound about like an untidy ribbon. The sun slipped away suddenly, plunging the earth into the darkest green twilight that Mike could remember. Then the rain came.

It was along a rutted path, slick with rain, that Dad, with obvious relief, brought the station wagon and trailer to an oozing stop.

Beyond the beam of the headlights was the incredible

darkness of the Colorado night. A play of lightning over the skyline lit a rambling house standing at the base of a deep, foreboding bluff.

"Well," Dad said tiredly, "we're here."

Elsie began to stretch awake. In doing so, she gouged her saddle shoe painfully into Mike's shin. He couldn't move away because the seat was packed too tightly with things Mother had forgotten to load in the trailer.

In the quiet of the car, he suddenly noticed a smell. It was the damp earth around the lilac plant . . . the earth of home. Mike was glad of the dark as he wiped a tear on his sleeve.

"That's all right," he told himself fiercely, "I'll run away, that's what I'll do, I'll run away home to Kansas."

2

RESPONSIBLE BOY WANTED

From the first morning that Mike wakened to the curious silence of their Colorado home, his homesickness grew steadily worse. Pulling the blanket about him because of the cool morning air, Mike padded to the window to look out.

The view from the window reminded him of something. The house was beside the road that led through a narrow valley. It stood so close to the rocky cliff that it seemed to have pulled itself back politely to let the road go by. Across the road lay a narrow field that quickly rose into the opposing mountain. Next to a field of neat, low green bushes, stood a neighboring house, the only house along the road that Mike could see.

The mountain that rose swiftly behind the house and field was studded with fir trees and aspen and, though the light was full, still hid the sun.

Mike was still staring out when Merrie came in, her heels slapping in the loose house shoes she had apparently borrowed from Mom.

"How does it look to you?" she asked cordially, joining him at the window.

"Like the pictures that hang in the first grade room on 'Go to School Night,' " he answered bluntly.

Merrie cocked her head, then laughed in agreement. "Can't argue with that," she said. "It's an up-and-down business, that's for sure. Don't you think it's pretty, though?"

Because Mike couldn't meet her eyes, he just shook his head slowly. "Not really, Merrie. It's too strange."

"I'm sorry, Mike," she said quietly.

"Maybe it'll look better after breakfast," he added quickly. "I'm starved."

Merrie winced, tightening her shoulders a minute. "Breakfast," she repeated out loud. "I'll go help Mom."

She turned at the door to give him a quick sideways grin. "You better dress and come, too. We'll need all hands."

At the door of the kitchen, Mike suddenly understood. Mom was down on the floor sitting on her heels, surrounded by cardboard boxes filled with groceries and canned goods that she had brought from the other house.

"I'll help," he offered, reaching for the nearest box.

Mother's hands flew up warningly. "Don't touch a thing," she warned. "I have this all organized. Every box is classified. I just have to find the right one, and we're set."

"Where's Dad?" Mike asked.

"Unloading the trailer," Mother replied absently.

Mike went to carry boxes in for Dad. As he set one down, he heard Mom still complaining.

"Somewhere there's a box with all the breakfast things. There's tomato juice and pancake mix and dried milk." She began to scramble furiously in a box, frowning as if this would help her find it.

Elsie leaned in the doorway staring at them through a pale veil of loose, uncombed hair. "I'm hungry," she said firmly.

"Mom is working on breakfast," Mike answered as his mother dived into the next box and studied its contents earnestly.

"I'm starving," Elsie added solemnly.

"Pancake mix, waffle syrup, butter, and canned sausage," Mother repeated determinedly, pushing one box aside to try another.

"I'm starving to death from hunger," Elsie repeated a little louder.

Mike took the tablecloth Merrie handed him and fitted it as well as he could on the table that was longer and not as wide as the one at home.

Mom was muttering unhappily and staring around the circle of boxes again.

Elsie began to wail. "I'm starving to death from hunger in my stomach," she complained loudly, banging her Teddy bear fiercely against the doorway.

"Maybe that box is still in the car," Mom suggested to no one in particular. She left, frowning, with Elsie trailing loudly behind her.

Merrie had poked about in the cupboard and found a blue tea kettle which she set to boil.

"I found it," Mom called triumphantly as she came

in with a box. Merrie laughed. She had the table set now, and oatmeal was bubbling little volcanoes of steam into the cool air of the kitchen.

"Where did that come from?" Mike asked as he passed the kitchen door carrying a box of boots.

"From a box marked *baking supplies*," Merrie said. "Also the brown sugar."

"Well, here's tomorrow's breakfast, anyway." Mom laughed, setting her precious cargo down. "I always get so confused in a new kitchen."

Mike brought milk from the cooler in the back of the station wagon, and they ate the hot oatmeal with brown sugar melted into delightful pools.

"The first of August will be here before we know it," Dad announced during breakfast. "Let's make the most of our time and see how settled we can get."

Mike set Mom's lilac in the dooryard first. Dad helped Mom and Merrie get the clothes into the right closets and Elsie's toys into her room. Mike reassembled Elsie's sandbox in the little back yard. When Dad brought sacks of sand from the lumber yard late that afternoon, Elsie seemed at home.

By bedtime, Mike did not really care where he was.

He was tired and strangely sleepy. He went to sleep halfway through the slow, thoughtful cry of an owl in the trees behind the house.

The next morning, after breakfast, Mike let Elsie trail along while he went to investigate the neighboring property.

The low bushes Mike had noticed that first morning grew all about the green house down the road. An old man was working among them. He watched soberly as Mike and Elsie approached, staring at them from under a tangled brush of gray eyebrows.

"They're gooseberries," he answered Mike matter-of-factly, as if even Elsie should have been able to figure that out.

Elsie studied them soberly as Mike explained. "They look like the ones that grow wild in Kansas, but I've never seen so many gooseberries before."

"Probably the best you'll ever see," the old man went on complacently.

"What do you do with them?" Elsie asked curiously.

"Sell them for my keeping money."

"Keeping money?" Mike asked.

"Like Jensen," the old man said, nodding toward

Mike and Elsie's house.

"I don't know about Jensen," Mike admitted as the man went back to curling a slim hoe in and about the weedless roots of the plants.

The hoe stopped as the man looked at Mike amazed.

"Laf Jensen. That's his house you folks live in. He's in Sweden now."

"Sweden," Mike said, surprised.

"All these years he's been saving his money," the man went on. "Laf always said everybody has a thing they want to do. So you keep some money aside and save it, and with that money you do what you really want, when you're ready. Laf got ready."

"But he's coming back someday?" Mike said with sudden hope. Maybe we'll move back home, he thought quickly. He had to laugh at his own silliness, remembering that it was Dad's new job that brought them here, not just Laf Jensen's empty house.

"He might and he might not." The old man shrugged.

"I have something I want to do," Mike said slowly. "But I need a job to earn money before I can do it."

The old man looked at him speculatively. "How old are you?"

"Eleven," Mike said, trying to look tall for it.

The man squinted at him thoughtfully. "You'll find it. You're big enough. Of course you can't be too dead set on what you're going to work at."

"Oh, I'm not," Mike replied hastily. "How would you begin if you were me?"

"Just go to town and ask around. Folks all know each other's business here."

Mom was delighted to give him permission to go down the hill to the main street. He had barely gotten his request out before she began looking about for a pencil and a piece of paper. "I have a little list in my head of things I need," she said. "And you can bring them."

As she handed him the list, she added, "I didn't put this down, but if you have a chance, ask someone what bird it is that sings as it flies. It's a small, black-colored bird that flashes white in flight."

"I'll try, Mom."

"If I didn't know better, I would be sure it was a sky-lark," Mom added thoughtfully. "This place is fantastic, don't you think, Mike?"

He only smiled and pocketed her note. "Black sky-lark, huh?"

:30

The walk to town was all downhill. Mike passed the school — a small, square building shut up for the summer — then a cluster of houses. That will be where the other kids live, he thought as he passed.

Maybe Mom's word was right. It was fantastic that any place could be so different from Wichita and only be one state away. The trees, the birds, even the dust was different. The little main street, which was the only business street of Goldstream, seemed to be out of a different time. There was a general store, a small post office tucked between the hardware store and a drugstore whose window was filled with bright bottles of colored liquid and a pair of copper scales. The buildings were not only very small, but they were completely different from the ones at home.

Instead of being great cubes of concrete and brick, the stores were more like tall wooden houses wearing the masks of outdated store fronts. Across the tops, false fronts that stuck up above the roof level were decorated with curlicues of wood and fancy trimmings. Each building bore a legend, carved in elaborate letters. Mike read them to himself, "Jonathan Budger, 1875; Mc-Quillen, 1901."

The people were all friendly. They showed a generous interest in Mike, and seemed not to mind being interrupted.

"No work, son," the inevitable answer came. "You must be the new boy from Jensen's Place?"

Mike finally nodded amiably at this question. There was no point in repeating his own name. He was the boy from Jensen's Place and that was that.

It was the editor of the *Bugle* who was the most helpful.

"No such thing as a paper delivery out here, son," he said. "Only a goat could manage the route, and anyway, the paper goes out by rural post, mostly. We'll put you on the mailing list for awhile and you watch the want ads. If you don't give up too easily, something might turn up."

After Mike bought Mom's groceries and was ready to start home, he went back to the *Bugle* office. "I have a funny question from my Mom," he told Mr. Crowley and asked him about the bird.

"She has the laugh on you, son," Mr. Crowley said. "That's the lark bunting, and its song is almost identical to the English skylark. It's our state bird. Looks like your mom is going to become a real Coloradian."

"Wait until you hear one sing," Mom said, when he delivered the groceries to her and told her what Mr. Crowley had said. "His song is as breath-taking as these mountains."

Merrie and Mike both watched for want ads in the papers that week and the next. Someone advertised for a companion for an elderly woman, and later, for a truck driver, but there were no openings for boys.

Once the family was settled in, Dad went off fishing for whole days and came back, glowing and happy, with strings of sleek rainbow trout.

"I wish you'd try this fly casting just once, Mike," Dad coaxed. "You couldn't help being caught by it."

Merrie giggled. "I tried it, and I was caught, but not the way you mean."

"I'm just no fisherman, I guess," Mike said. He felt bad about it inside, but the idea of splashing all afternoon up and down a stream with a fishing rod just didn't sound reasonable when you could be doing something like throwing a baseball or even practicing basketball shots at the loop against the garage.

Mike felt that he was only marking time. In his mind, he was using Mr. Jensen's phrase. He was looking for a job to earn "keeping money." When he had enough, he could use it to run away home. On his long hikes of exploration on the wooded mountain that rose behind the house, he tried to plan how it would be when he got back to Wichita. A visit wouldn't do, he wanted to go there for good. If he once got there, surely some of his friends, maybe their neighbors the Prentices, someone would let him stay with them and go to school. Then Mom and Dad wouldn't worry. He could work evenings and buy his own clothes. And Merrie would be close, right there at the University. She could write them that he was fine, if they got worried. The first thing to do was make enough money to get back, then the rest would work out.

The day the ad appeared, Mike ran to Merrie breathlessly carrying the paper. Spreading it out in front of her, he pressed it flat. "Look here, Sis," he said. "What do you think?"

Merrie read it, twisting a loose curl thoughtfully. "Responsible boy wanted," she read slowly, "to care for three kids for three weeks. Food bill plus salary. Orr's End."

"Baby-sitting?" Merrie asked incredulously.

"I'm in no position to be choosy," Mike answered.

"Besides, it says right here, 'Boy.' And I've taken care of Elsie a lot."

Merrie stared at him a moment, her eyes wide, then she grinned. "Anyway, I could help if it got rough."

"Think I ought to check with Mom?"

"Probably," Merrie agreed hesitantly, "but she's all involved in organizing a sewing room so she can finish my college clothes. Why don't you just go check where Orr's End is, and find out more about it before bothering her?"

Mike was halfway to town when Bucky, his shepherd, caught up with him. The big dog galloped about him, panting happily.

"Not this time, Boy," Mike told him. "Go home."

Mike finally abandoned his efforts to make Bucky return. He led the dog back to the house and fastened his chain.

"Let him go in a little while, will you, Merrie?"

Mike laughed. Bucky drooped on the lawn as if he were heartbroken. "Business trips are different, fellow," Mike told him, patting his head before starting off down the road again.

It seemed logical to Mike to check the address with the editor of the *Bugle*.

Mr. Crowley grinned broadly, wiping his inky fingers on his apron. "I thought about you when I set that ad for Mr. Orr," he said. "More power to you. Come outside. I'll point you in the right direction."

Mike listened carefully, then repeated the directions back to Mr. Crowley. "One mountain looks just like another one to me," he explained.

Mr. Crowley laughed. "You'll make no mistake, son. Orr's End is like nothing else in these parts."

The amusement behind Mr. Crowley's last words spurred Mike as he wheeled his bike around the turn that led off behind the feed store. Added to his interest in the job was a new curiosity. What was so different and funny about Mr. Orr . . . and Orr's End?

3

RICK, TICK, AND TAWNY

Mr. Crowley's directions led Mike out of town on a road he had never followed. Wheeling along, just a little ways past the end of the business district, Mike stopped his bike suddenly and sniffed the air.

It smelled like home . . . home in Wichita. But it was not an afternoon smell, it was a scent he associated with warm summer evenings. As he rounded the bend, the smell was explained.

A big lumber installation spread over what looked like two city blocks. There was a cluster of buildings and neat stacks of finished wood. In the background stood a strange building, shaped rather like a tepee without a door. From a black hole in its top came a slow curl of sweet white smoke. It was a charcoal pile. No wonder it smelled like dinnertime in Wichita. The only thing needed to make it complete was a hamburger grill stuck over the top.

Because the surrounding mountains shielded the deep valley from wind, the smoke rose lazily, like an indolent genie reluctant to rise to freedom.

Once past the lumber company, the road began to steepen quickly. Mike finally got off his bike and walked beside it.

The joke must be about where the house was. It did seem funny to have a place set that far up the rocky grade. There wasn't a sign of human life between town and Orr's End. The trees along the road flashed with the scarlet and black of red-winged blackbirds garnering nuts from the cones in the tall trees. Off among the slender pines, a woodpecker tapped a riotous rhythm in the deep shade.

Finally, with a sigh of relief, Mike saw a stone wall surrounding a solid mass of blue spruce trees. A chimney poked above the treetops and, by a rustic gate, was a simple sign.

"Orr's End," Mike read aloud with satisfaction. He leaned his bike against the wall, and pushed the gate open. He was startled by a voice speaking companionably almost in his ear.

"You must have come about my ad. You're the new boy in town," a man's voice said cordially.

Mike looked at the man, and then at the house again. In the split second after he entered the gate and before the man spoke, Mike had caught a glimpse of the house. It was like the very nicest houses back in Wichita. It was fashioned of gray rock with stucco and rich dark wooden beams crisscrossed between tall, formal windows. It wasn't at all the house he expected to find on the mountaintop.

"Yes, sir," Mike said as quickly as he could recover. He tried not to stare at the faded, shabby plaid shirt and the rough trousers tucked into knee boots. Mr. Orr looked, for all the world, like a very old and down-on-his-luck prospector who had been left out in the sun too long.

The hand he thrust out to Mike was short and broad with hard callouses that scraped Mike's hand.

"I'm Bert Orr," the man said. "Do you want the job?"

"I came to see about it," Mike answered slowly. "I've

never really done any work like this before."

"I didn't specify experience," Mr. Orr replied. "But I need a responsible boy who isn't already tied up with other work. These are very special kids, you know."

Mike almost frowned, trying to picture the children who would live in this house and belong to this man.

"I'm sure they are, sir," Mike replied uneasily.

Mr. Orr motioned Mike to follow and went on talking. "The reason they're so special is their mother," he said gruffly. He stopped suddenly to stare intensely at Mike. "You do understand they're orphaned?"

"Well, no, sir. I'm real sorry." Mike began helplessly, rather surprised at the man's terse tone.

"Wonderful creature, their mother," Mr. Orr went on, walking briskly ahead again. "But no sense at all about rocks. She, herself, started the rock slide that killed her."

"Gosh!" Mike was horrified. "How terrible!"

"She started it herself," Mr. Orr said firmly, as if her awkwardness made the loss more bearable.

As Mr. Orr stopped, Mike realized that they had come through the trees to an immense wire fence. Although Mike knew that Mr. Orr was watching him, he still couldn't resist staring. "Kids," he repeated numbly. He

stared back through the fence at three small bearded faces that studied him with clear yellow eyes. The goat in the middle asked gently, "Baaaa?"

"That's Tick," Mr. Orr said fondly. "She's always the most polite — when you're looking."

"Kids," Mike repeated numbly. All sorts of things began to fall into place . . . their mother . . . the rock slide. "Gosh, they're cute," he said, smiling up at Mr. Orr. One goat lifted a dainty foot and scratched delicately behind his ear.

Mr. Orr grinned broadly. "The black-and-white one is Rick and the dark one is Tawny. They're pretty great."

Mike was busy rearranging his thoughts as Mr. Orr went on. "I'm going East to visit my family this summer. First time I've gone since I started keeping goats. I need someone to take care of them the three weeks I will be gone. It seems like every boy in town either has a job or helps his folks out at home. I took a chance on finding someone with that ad."

He paused, then asked brusquely. "Now that you have seen them, do you want the job?"

Mike struggled for words. All sorts of problems suddenly presented themselves. Things he would have to

ask Mom and Dad about . . . and as for Merrie helping. . . .

"Seven dollars a week plus all they eat," Mr. Orr went
on, "and I supply the fence. Don't figure anyone wants
to come up this hill twice a day to feed them."

Mike nodded agreement. He grinned with sudden
delight. This would be fun, if Mom and Dad would
only. . . .

"Can't imagine your folks not approving. That is,
unless they have enough work lined up for you to do?"

Mike shook his head. "I just have little things around
the house — mowing the lawn, for instance. I have lots
of extra time."

Mr. Orr looked thoughtful. "You *are* responsible,
aren't you?" Mr. Orr asked this a little worriedly, peer-
ing intently at Mike.

"I try to be," Mike answered.

"Well, you see, these aren't just goats . . . they're special kids."

"Yes, sir," Mike replied, confused.

"If they were just goats, I could sell them and buy
new ones next fall, but these are special goats because of
their mother. You understand that?"

"No, sir," Mike replied honestly.

Mr. Orr looked startled before laughing suddenly at Mike's frankness. His deep, loud laugh was startling coming from such an old man.

"Well, it's not a long story, really," Mr. Orr said with relish. "I used to have some mines around this country — silver mines. I came up here as a young prospector with nothing but my strength and my grubstake and a goat that I traded a fellow an old gun for. Goats are good company, and the milk filled out my meals a little.

"I was having nothing but bad luck until one day that silly old goat got herself caught in a cave. I went in and picked away some rock to set her free and made my first strike. I kept her until she died and then her daughter and then her daughter's daughter. I sort of felt they were my lucky pieces. Then, last winter, the mother of this set of triplets started the rock slide that killed her. They're the last of the line."

"Do you still run the mines, sir?" Mike asked curiously.

"Land, no, son. They ran out years ago, and the men who worked them got jobs in Denver making planes. They wear out, mines do, but I was about ready to retire anyway, so it didn't matter too much."

"They're sure cute," Mike said, watching the one called Rick reaching delicately through the fence to nibble at Mr. Orr's pocket.

"He's the brave one," Mr. Orr grinned. "His whole name is Richard Lionheart. Tick is for Ticonderoga, and Tawny is just because she is. Now what have you decided?" he asked brusquely. "As I said, I supply the fencing. Mr. Owens over at the bank will mail you a check every Friday, and you order out their feed from the General Store and have it put on my bill."

"But my parents," Mike said. "I really. . . ."

Mr. Orr slapped his shoulder genially. "Nobody with a fine boy like you would object to three little goats. Where did you say you lived?"

"Jensen's place," Mike answered absently.

"We ought to get this settled right away," Mr. Orr went on briskly. "You hop on home with your bike, and I'll see you later."

"Yes, sir," Mike answered and turned towards the gate again, his head full of fuzzy questions.

He had taken only one step before the gentle sound came again. Tick's head cocked at him impudently. She chewed vigorously for a minute, then asked, "Baaaa?"

Mike winked at her, feeling suddenly excited. If Mom and Dad only agreed, this might be a very entertaining way to earn his "keeping" money.

:46

Mike whistled to himself as he left the gate to start down the winding hill towards town. "Rick, Tick, and Tawny," he repeated to himself, chuckling at Merrie's coming reaction. He could easily imagine Merrie baby-sitting, but kid tending was something different.

He must have looked pretty silly wheeling out of Mr. Orr's drive, grinning like a jack-o-lantern. He almost passed the boy before he saw him. He was about Mike's height, maybe a little taller, but not much. The way he was dressed, in blue jeans and a T-shirt, made Mike suddenly conscious of his own Bermuda shorts.

The look he was giving Mike was anything but friendly.

"Well, hi," Mike said in surprise.

The boy, who Mike was later to learn was Brad Mitchell, ignored the greeting.

"I guess you got the job," he said curtly.

Mike was at a loss. "I guess so," he almost stammered.

"What kind of an answer is that?" the boy sneered, looking Mike up and down derisively. "You either did or you didn't."

"I haven't checked with my folks," Mike said.

The boy simpered an insulting smile. "Don't keep

47:

me from going home and asking Mommy," he said in
an artificial tone. "I didn't really want the old job anyway," the boy muttered. "My dad keeps me more than
busy enough."

Mike was stunned. He stared after the boy who
snapped onto a black bike and wheeled off rapidly.

"I ought to go after him," he thought. But then, that
would be one great way to get started in a town . . . chase
down a kid you don't even know and make him fight you.

Mostly it hurt. Mike looked down at his Bermuda
shorts and shook his head. Come to think of it, he hadn't
seen any other fellows in shorts.

It was simple enough to quit wearing shorts, he told
himself. But how simple would it be to convince Mom
that it would be fun to have a goat pen and three lively
kids in the back yard? By the time he got to the news-
paper office, the excitement of the possible job was up-
permost in his mind again. He waved at Mr. Crowley
who was visiting in the doorway with another man.

In spite of the questioning grin on the editor's face,
Mike saw no point in stopping. Mike couldn't tell him
what he was going to do until he had Mom and Dad's
permission anyway.

By the time Mike got home, he was thirsty and his

throat was raw from the long, hot ride.

Merrie was curled up in a lawn chair by Elsie's sandbox when he skidded his bike to a stop. Merrie smiled up at him, closing her book on her finger. "How about the job?" she asked excitedly. "I could hardly wait until you got back to hear."

Mike laughed. "I can hardly wait to tell you." He slid off the bike. "But I'm dying of thirst. I'll be right out."

Mom must have been listening for Mike, too. As he entered the kitchen, she called down from her room, "Mike, will you do me a favor?"

"Sure, Mom," he answered, setting down his glass of water to go upstairs.

Her bedroom was strewn with bright fabrics and little piles of sewing supplies.

Mom handed him a list written on a torn piece of envelope. Attached to it was a strip of bright pink cloth.

"I ran out of thread and can't locate my narrow elastic. If you would wheel to town for these things, it would mean I could do the hand work on this outfit of Merrie's this evening while we sit around. You don't mind? It isn't too hot, is it?"

"No," Mike replied. He hesitated a minute, wanting to tell her about his job. Her obvious desire to get the supplies and get back to her sewing made this seem like a bad time to ask permission.

He did take enough time to slip out of his shorts and put on jeans. "Just in case I see that boy again," he told himself.

"I have to make a quick trip for Mom," he told Merrie who was still in the yard watching Elsie. "I'll tell you when I get back."

At the bottom of the list, Mike saw an added item. "Chocolate soda for the errand boy," it said. He grinned and stuck the package of sewing things in his pocket. That was the kind of mom to have, the kind that couldn't finish her work unless her boy had a chocolate soda right before supper.

Mike hurried after he left the drugstore. It was nearly time for Dad to get home, and Mike was anxious to ask him about his job.

As Mike turned in the drive at home, he saw a red truck backed into the drive ahead of him. Merrie and Elsie were staring wide-eyed at a man who was briskly unloading things from the truck. By the time Mike reached him, there were two immense bales of wire, a keg of staples, and a stack of posts already piled at the end of the drive.

On their leashes, tied in the back of the truck, Rick, Tick, and Tawny danced about unhappily. Elsie was on tiptoes, squealing and trying to see them better. Merrie stood dumfounded, her book hanging limply in her hand.

"Where shall I tie them for now?" the man called to Mike, as he lifted the kids onto the ground, holding their leashes firmly.

Mike didn't get a chance to tell him. He had forgotten one member of the family. His big shepherd dog, Bucky, loped around the house to investigate the noise. He stopped stiff-legged, staring at Rick, Tick, and Tawny who were prancing nervously just a rope length from the delivery man.

Bucky crouched and started towards them. Knowing Bucky, Mike knew it was only his half-fearful way of getting close enough to investigate, but Rick, Tick, and Tawny didn't understand. With a wild chorus of an-guished bleating, they tried to escape. They ran wildly around the delivery man so that he was quickly cocooned with rope. As the ropes broke from their collars, the man fell, rolling down the driveway like a poor loser in a sack race.

Elsie giggled happily as Rick, Tick, and Tawny, blocked from escape by the truck and the garage, ran to the house and leaped to the sill of the dining room window, turning their backs on Bucky and bleating with terror.

"Better catch them," the delivery man warned. "If they get off, they're gone."

Talking gently, Mike and Merrie approached the window and lifted the terrified kids down.

"In the garage, Merrie," Mike called. "We can keep them in there until we figure out what to do."

In the sudden quiet that followed the closing of the garage doors, Mike was suddenly filled with dismay.

"Whatever is Dad going to say?" he asked Merrie.

"Here he comes now," she replied as the station wagon turned in the drive. Dad pulled over to leave room for the red truck to get out.

"Can I help you, sir?" Dad asked curiously, staring from the stack of supplies to the driver who was still dusting himself off before getting back into his truck.

"Everything seems fine now," the man said blandly. "I'm from McKay's Lumber Yard, and I delivered the kids for Mr. Orr when I brought this other stuff," he explained.

Dad looked puzzled.

"Kids?" he asked, looking confusedly at Mike, Merrie, and Elsie who had come to greet him.

"Goats," Mike said with a gulp. "I took a job baby-sitting some kid goats for a man who is going to take a trip, and they came today."

"In the garage," Merrie explained.

Mike hadn't meant to tumble it all out like this. He was suddenly terribly scared. It had been a poor start for sure. He looked at Dad hopefully. "I hope it's all right, Dad?"

"Well, they're here now." Dad grinned, giving him a friendly shove. "You might as well give it a try."

Dad turned thoughtfully to the delivery man who was getting back into his truck.

"Who is this Mr. Orr? Is he in the goat milk business or something?"

The man looked up startled before laughing out loud. "Mr. Orr? He's probably the richest man in Gold-stream. He made a fortune in silver mining and he is superstitious about goats!" He grinned. "Awful nice old fellow . . . just a little silly about goats, that's all."

With that, he crawled into the truck, set its motor to coughing, and pulled out.

"Well, son," Dad grinned. "We better go have supper and get your kids penned up."

"Where is Mom anyway?" Merrie asked. "It's a wonder she's not out here with all this confusion."

They found her standing in the dining room still staring dazedly at the windows.

"Something wrong?" Dad asked as they all looked at her from the doorway.

"I don't know," she said unhappily. "I, uh . . . I was in the closet looking for a box and thought I heard something in the drive. When I got to the window there were. . . ." She flushed and stopped with her hand in front of her mouth as if she were afraid to go on.

Merrie began to giggle. "What did you see, Mom?" she asked.

"Don't you dare laugh!" Mom said defensively. "I saw . . . well, it looked like three little bearded men."

Dad reached over and gave her a quick hug. "That must have given you a start. Those are Mike's little kids. Let's go and have supper. I think we all need it."

4

GIRLS! AND THEIR IDEAS!

Nobody dared to kid Mom very much during dinner, but Mike could tell from Dad's sly grin that he wanted to.

Elsie ate so rapidly that Mom had to keep reminding her to slow down.

"I'm 'skited," she told Mom. "We got kids."

"Excited," Mom corrected, "and it looks as if they will be around a while."

"Right after dinner can I go see?" Elsie asked.

"You'll have to wait until Mike and I get the fence built," Dad explained. "Do you want our windows full of dwarfs again?"

Merrie winked at Mike as Mom said firmly, "That's enough, Bob."

Mike and Dad hurried with dinner, postponing dessert to get the job done while some light was left.

Elsie's attempts to help kept interrupting their work until Mike finally stopped and constructed a teeter-totter for her from the nail keg and a board he found in the garage.

Merrie helped Elsie balance a whole family of dolls on one end, and Elsie played happily while Mike and Dad set the posts and stretched the wire for the little goat pen.

By the time they had finished, the sun had disappeared, and only a soft, warm glow of light played along the edge of the bluffs. Mike carefully opened the garage door and herded the goats into their enclosure.

They entered meekly, staring about with their little bright eyes. While Tawny sampled the water, Rick stared about belligerently. Tick stood just inside the gate.

"Baaa," Mike bleated reassuringly. Tick trotted into the yard happily as Dad shook his head grinning.

Mom had come out to watch. "They really are cute."

She said it very firmly as if she were trying to convince herself.

Elsie clung to the fence staring in at the kids, breathless with excitement.

"That seesaw was sure a good idea, Mike," Dad commented. "Remind me to bring it out of the pen tomorrow. Elsie will have lots of fun with it. Now I'll have my dessert," he said, catching Mom by the arm.

By the time Mike finished his ice cream, Mom had Elsie in her sleepers. Mike went to the back door to look out at the kids. There were peculiar sounds coming from the pen. Mike went closer to investigate. A fingernail of a moon had risen brightly... the pale light shone intermittently on the snowy beards of the goats. There was a click, click, click, click, then a thud. Then it would begin again — click, click, click, click, thud. As Mike drew near the fence, he watched in amazement. He rubbed his eyes and stared a minute before running back to the house as quietly as he could.

"Hey, Mom, Dad, Merrie, Elsie," he whispered urgently into the kitchen. "Come quickly, but be quiet!"

Although they came almost silently, Mike realized that noise wouldn't have mattered. The three goats were like boys in a tight marble game. They were too busy to hear thunder.

They were playing on the seesaw, their little hooves making a click, click, click on the wooden plank.

Tawny ran up first with Rick and Tick following close behind. As Tawny and Rick passed the center of the board, where it rested on the keg, the board would be thrown off balance. Tick, caught behind them on the rising board would be thrown into the air, her white beard waving nobly in the moonlight. Tick would no sooner land on the ground than the three would turn and race up the seesaw again.

Mom and Dad laughed helplessly. Elsie giggled so wildly that Mom finally took her into bed, fearful that she would never be able to settle down to sleep if she became any more amused.

After Mike was in bed, Dad came in and sat on the edge of his bed.

"Well, son, it looks as if your bearded vaudeville team is going to be fun to have around."

Mike grinned, feeling suddenly closer to Dad than he had since the move. "I'm sure glad, Dad. I was worried there for a while."

"So was I," Dad admitted. They listened for a minute to the click of the goats still enjoying the teeter-totter before Dad rumpled Mike's hair and went back in to join Mom with her lapful of pink sewing.

Mike need not have worried about selling Dad on the idea of the kid-tending job. Rick, Tick, and Tawny did that for him.

Every day when Dad passed their fence, he stopped to play with them a minute or exchange a few friendly "Baas" with Tick.

Mom was unexpectedly happy about them, too. As long as the goats romped behind the fence, or came to nibble grass from her hand, Elsie played in the yard happily with no thought of straying or getting into mischief.

The days went swiftly. Dad was working on a regular schedule. Mom and Merrie busied themselves with preparations for Merrie's departure for the University.

The big event of every day was the mail delivery. Everyone stopped what he was doing and they gathered on the lawn chairs to trade mail. Mom would read snatches of letters from her friends in Wichita while Mike read the *Eagle*, especially the sports page where daily listings of the Little League baseball teams were posted in a special box.

Even though she got letters from her friends, day after day Merrie fussed with impatience as she sorted through the mail. She was waiting eagerly for a letter about a job in the college bookstore. It seemed that it was never going to come.

Merrie danced with joy the day the letter was delivered.

"What does it say?" Mike asked curiously.

Merrie giggled. "I haven't opened it yet," she realized with a start, tearing the envelope excitedly. "But just getting it makes me excited."

Mom and Mike watched her nod as she read the letter. Then a quick frown creased her face.

"Bad news?" Mom asked puzzled.

Merrie shook her head. "Not really. I did get the job. But I have to go about three weeks earlier than I planned."

"Lucky duck," Mike said, almost to himself.

Merrie looked at him thoughtfully.

"I guess I should be happy, but I hate to leave here. It's a long time until the first vacation."

Mike said nothing more, but he surely couldn't understand it. Just give him a chance to go back to Wichita.

He wouldn't care about vacations or anything. Listening to the scraps of news that Mom and Merrie shared from their correspondence always made him more desolate and lonely than before. He could always imagine the places and the friends they mentioned, and he hungered for the different sky of Kansas, the wide, blue prairie sky, crisscrossed by planes and the whipped shreds of summer clouds.

"I can't wait to tell Dad about my job," Merrie said happily. "Isn't it wonderful?"

"Yeah, I guess," Mike said. "But with all your studies and football games to go to and all, why did you want a job so bad?"

Merrie stared at him almost unbelieving. "You . . . of all people. Why, Mike, don't you remember how anxious you were before you got the kids? Why did you want a job so much?"

Mike felt himself coloring under her direct glance. He couldn't tell her the real truth. He only shrugged. "I'm a boy," he said vaguely.

She laughed. "And I'm a girl. That doesn't mean I can't be a help to Mom and Dad, does it?"

"Of course not," Mike mumbled. "I'm glad about your job."

"The only thing is that I'll have to go earlier than I'd planned." She mused. "But a week or two won't make that much difference."

Mike wasn't really listening any more. Two weeks had passed swiftly. Mike cashed the checks that came each week from the bank, and kept the money in his special cigar box. Sometimes, when he was cleaning the kids' pen, he would stop a minute and shut his eyes. That way, he could almost see the line of lights that marked the edge of the ball field back home. He could imagine the chorus of cries as the townspeople cheered the Majestic Laundry team on to victory. This suddenly seemed very different from Merrie's desire to "help Mom and Dad."

The only member of the family who didn't like the kids was Bucky. He stalked about the yard stiff-legged, looking very offended.

"You're just jealous, old fellow," Mike told him, rubbing the shepherd behind the ears. "They're just too popular for you."

"They tease him," Merrie explained, looking up from the lawn chair.

"Oh, Merrie," Mike grinned. "How can fenced goats tease a dog?"

Merrie nodded wisely. "You watch sometime. They really do."

Elsie looked up from her sand shovel. "They really do," she echoed wisely.

Mike laughed and threw a stick for Bucky to retrieve. Girls and their ideas!

Merrie marked the days of August off on the kitchen calendar. One week, two, finally the third week was growing to a close. Dad enjoyed his job almost as much as he enjoyed the weekends. He and Mom seemed younger and happier than Mike could ever remember.

"It's this place," Mom tried to explain. "Something about the air. I just think it's fantastic. I really do."

It seemed fantastic to Mike that his three-week job was almost over. Mr. Orr was due back on Sunday to pick up the kids. That last Saturday evening, Merrie was inside helping Mom finish up dinner while Mike ran the power mower in the front yard. The vibration of the motor filled the air about him. He heard the barking and the other strange sounds only dimly over the whir of his machine. Gradually, he realized they were strange and different noises. He made only a couple more runs the length of the brief front lawn before turning off the motor to go and check.

As he rounded the back yard, the sounds were already growing fainter. There was no one in the back yard at all. He could still hear the barking and the bleating of goats, but it sounded frighteningly far away.

"Elsie," he called. She had been there with Bucky and the kids only a few minutes before. She would know where they were.

He banged at the back door yelling, "Mom, Merrie, where's Elsie?"

They both came out instantly and stared at the open gate of the goat pen and the empty back yard.

"Never mind," Mike yelled. There was only one way Elsie could have gone without passing the front yard. He ran toward the cliff and began to scale it quickly. He worked along the shallow edges of rocks that almost formed a natural stairway.

Merrie was yelling, "Wait, wait," but Mike knew he must not. Bucky's barking was fading rapidly. Mike was sure that if the dog got out of sight in the hills behind the house, he would have no idea where to search.

Having reached the top of the cliff, Mike sighed with relief. He could see Elsie now, her red sweater a bright spot against the green grass. She was running rapidly towards the wooded area.

She stopped and waited when he called to her, waving her arms and crying bitterly. She was wailing so heart-brokenly that Mike couldn't make out her words even when he drew near.

Upon reaching her, he knelt beside her.

"Mike, I so sorry," she wailed against him. "Those kids teased Bucky something awful! I was going in to spank them and make them stop. They knocked me down and ran outside. Bucky is chasing them away."

Mike stroked her hair, wiping her face on his shirt. Merrie had almost caught up with them now. "Wait with Merrie, and don't worry," Mike told Elsie. "I'll find them."

"But you can't go alone," Merrie insisted, holding Elsie tightly against her shoulder.

"I'll follow Bucky's barking, it won't be hard," Mike said. "The kids are my responsibility," he added glumly.

Bucky's barking was Mike's only clue as to which direction to take. A craggy plateau lay beneath the next upward thrust of the mountain. Beyond the tip of it, Mike could see the afternoon sun tilting lazily behind a fringe of firs.

To follow the barking would be to follow the sun.

That would be west, Mike told himself, frighteningly conscious of the unending sameness of the pine woods. If he should lose sight of the rooftops of home, he could be lost until dawn came.

There was a sudden stillness as Mike entered the grove of trees. The barking seemed as separate from this place as sounds of another world would be. Even his feet made no crunching on the carpet of needles that covered the ground.

Mike called Bucky with all the strength of his voice. Once he thought the barking was fainter. Then, as it grew suddenly louder, Mike raced through the woods that were still greenly bright with afternoon light. It was then he realized, with horror, that Bucky might come at his call. He must follow the sounds only, or he would never find Rick, Tick, and Tawny.

Mike dropped his pace to a slow even trot. He passed a little stream that wandered brightly through the woods, its waters icy from the snow water that was its source.

Soon the woods grew thicker. There was no path at all in this uncleared stand of fir trees.

"Bucky," Mike called hesitatingly. The answering bark seemed very near, and yet somehow hollow.

"Bucky," he called again, louder. He strained to locate the source of the sound.

He had almost given up when Bucky suddenly appeared, as if from nowhere. The big shepherd dog shook himself briskly, deluging Mike with a spray of icy water.

"Where were you, boy?" Mike asked urgently, "and where are the kids?" Bucky whined and licked Mike's hand guiltily.

With a sinking heart, Mike realized from the fading light that he had almost no time to search before dark would fall.

Dad patted his shoulder encouragingly when Mike and Bucky had made their way back down the cliff.

"Nothing will happen to them tonight," he assured Mike. "With a good early start, you'll find them quickly . . . and safely, too."

"Maybe they'll come home alone," Merrie suggested.

Mike grinned. That was a good dream, anyway.

5

THE OTHER SIDE OF THE HILL

Mike wakened from his uneasy sleep with a sense of urgency. Faint tatters of dawn were trailing across the eastern sky, and the room was cold. They would never believe this back in Wichita, he thought glumly, shivering into his clothes. Imagine needing a sweat shirt on an August morning, even at dawn.

He took an apple from the fruit bowl on the kitchen table as he tiptoed through. Breakfast would have to wait until the goats were home. He let himself out silently into the rising morning, a rope in his hands.

Bucky stretched himself awake as Mike passed through

the yard. He yawned widely and started after Mike.

"Not on your life, fellow," Mike said. "You aren't going to start them off again, when — and if — I find them."

With Bucky scratching his objections loudly from inside the garage, Mike started up the face of the mountain. As soon as the sun was up, his directions would be certain. In any case, he was sure of his way until he reached the deep woods.

Strangely, the air got warmer as Mike ascended the mountain. He was already at the level of the plateau before the sun really rose enough to start dispersing the threads of fog that draped the mountains.

As before, time lost its meaning once he was within the deep woods. Rounding a big tree, he startled a doe grazing with her fawn. She turned and fled, leaping first to the left and then to the right, as her fawn, its over-large ears stiffly erect, bounced along after her. An impossible stillness fell after the last echo of their crashing flight died.

From the position of the sun, Mike knew he was still going west. Maybe it was a mistake not to have brought Bucky. Maybe Bucky would remember the way and lead him. It was too late to worry about that now. Mike walked slowly, looking this way and that for the trail marks that he had so hastily assembled in last night's growing darkness.

In spite of his watchfulness, he almost passed his marker. It was in a clearing to his left. Only by chance, his eye followed the flight of a startled bird and saw the awkward wooden trail sign he had made on the needled ground.

He was here. But where was he? It was into this clearing that Bucky had bounded, dripping with icy water. Perhaps there was a stream, but how could he be sure which way the goats had gone?

Counting his steps, Mike went first south, then north, and finally west of the clearing. He found nothing . . . no stream, no pool, nothing that would suggest which way the three wide-eyed runaways had gone. It could not be due east, for that was how he had come.

Mike peered into the thicket thoughtfully and bleated in the best imitation he could muster of Tick's companionable cry.

He could have imagined that faint echo. Even if it had come, he could not have been sure. A huge red squirrel was chattering defiance at Mike's entry into this private place. The squirrel's grating recital of complaint would have drowned out any timid sound.

"All right, hush," he called to the squirrel. But it only flattened itself high against the trunk of a pine tree and switched its tail in an angry accompaniment to its chattering.

When the creature wouldn't be quiet, Mike pulled a small stick from his trail marker and threw it against the tree to drive the noisy chatterer away. This worked. The squirrel poured a torrent of reproach at Mike as it sped along the high branch, leaped to the other side of the tree, and made a rapid departure towards the northeast.

Mike listened to it go, puzzled. There had been something like an echo again, this time repeating the rat-a-tat of squirrel rebuke.

Carefully, Mike walked in the direction that the squirrel had gone. He bleated softly, then listened. He was right. There was an echo. But what in this green, deep place was throwing his voice back at him? He pricked his hands on the stiff needles of fur shrubs as he forced them apart to search. Suddenly, from almost beneath his nose, a faint bleat sounded. It sounded like an echo that had gotten lost and had finally been found again. Frantically, Mike pushed the bushes apart. He

found a small, still pool surrounded by great piles of rock. Above it arched a rocky opening shaped like a half-moon. The pool was deep, and the glint of fish caught the light in its depths.

Mike slipped his hand into the water. It was icy. Surely, this was where Bucky had gotten wet. This small opening must be the mouth of an underground river. Lying on his stomach, Mike stared into the dark cavern that led into the mountain. What he wouldn't give for a flashlight!

Suddenly, a small set of angled yellow lights glowed along the wall of the cave, then another, and yet another. Before he could accustom his eyes to the darkness of the cave, one pair of bright eyes winked at him slowly and asked, like a tender question, "Baaaa?"

"Tick," Mike cried in relief. But what in the world was a goat doing in that river? The yellow eyes rose and, with a click of small hooves, neared him.

Only slowly did Mike comprehend. The river had cut a large cave beyond this small opening. Along its sides ran a shelf, rather like a walkway. This was wide enough for the goats to lie down on and sleep. How he wished for a light! Even a match would light this place for an instant.

Tick was at the opening now. She leaped daintily from the ledge into the water. As she brought herself up on the bank, she showered Mike with icy water, shaking herself dry.

The other two goats were following her. Mike had a ridiculous desire to go back and explore the cave even though he realized that, without a light, he would be able to see little more than he could from the opening.

Rick and Tawny plunged through the pool as Tick had done. Mike, drenched and cold, glowed with relief as they clattered about him.

"All right, you mischief-boxes," he said affectionately, scratching each of their hard, knobby heads in turn, "let's go home."

He did not need the rope he had brought. The goats accompanied him almost eagerly. Sometimes they ran ahead, bouncing in springy circles about him. When they stopped to graze, he waited. The sun was high and warm by the time they reached the plateau. His sweat shirt steamed, and he fought off a dulling sleepiness.

"Come on, kids," he yelled at them. "Let's go." He ran across the open space as fast as he could go. They raced with him, circling him happily, teasing him with their greater speed. They leaped sure-footedly down

the cliff as Mike followed carefully, setting his feet sideways on the rocky slope.

His family had heard his whooping cries from the
cliff above. They stood in the back yard, shading their
eyes and watching his approach with obvious relief.

"Who brought who home?" Dad asked, grinning, as
he opened the pen gate and shooed the frisky goats inside. They entered meekly, then rushed towards their
feeding trough hungrily.

"The point is they are all here," Mom said thankfully.

"Where did you find them?" Merrie asked curiously.

"West and north of here," Mike said, "in a cave where
an underground river comes out."

Dad whistled. "You were lucky."

Mike nodded. "I sure was. I guess you've had breakfast," he added wistfully.

"Oh, Mike," Mom said contritely. "Of course, you're
hungry." She went in the house and, almost immediately,
the smell of sizzling bacon began to tease the air.

"West and north," Dad mused aloud. "That would
make it right above Orr's End, wouldn't it?"

"I guess it would," Mike agreed thoughtfully. "But
the woods are so deep there that you have to be right on
top of a thing before you see it."

"One egg or two?" Mom called from the back door.

"Three," Mike called back, and went in to wash for breakfast.

By the time he had finished eating, Mike's eyes were half shut. "I'm going to take a nap," he announced yawning. "If Mr. Orr comes, wake me up."

He saw the quick glance pass between Merrie and his parents.

"What's the matter?" he asked quickly.

"Nothing, son, but you know, you had better say good-by to Merrie before you bunk in. We'll be taking her to the station right after lunch."

Mike stared. This really hadn't registered on him. He had listened to the increasing talk of Merrie's plans about the University, he had seen the trunk packed, and shared in her elation when she had received confirmation of a job in the college bookstore. Not until now had it really dawned on him that the end of August, the end of his responsibility for the goats, and the end of Merrie's time with them all came on the same day — today.

"But Merrie," he protested, "it can't be time yet. So soon."

"I know, Mike, but my job in the bookstore starts this week." She shook her head. "It sneaked up on me, too." She leaned over and scrubbed his head hard with her knuckles. "I'm not leaving the world you know — I'll be just a state away."

"A state away," Mike thought numbly. That was what Wichita was, but it seemed more like a world.

"I want to go see you off," he said. "I'm not as sleepy as I thought I was."

Dad frowned. "I sure hate to be this way, son, but if Mr. Orr came while you were gone, it wouldn't be very fair."

Mike considered this with a grimace. "Okay, I'll stay," he said unhappily. "But I'm not going to take any old nap, then."

"You had better, boy." Merrie laughed at him. "You're the worst looking brother I've ever had."

Mike laughed. Then he realized with astonishment that her eyes weren't laughing at all, only her mouth was. "Jeepers," he thought "you don't suppose she's going to bawl?"

He punched her arm hard as he passed her chair. "See you Thanksgiving, Sis. And learn something, will you?"

She hit back at him and missed. He dodged and ran

off up the stairs. If his own eyes felt strangely moist, it was nobody's business!

Mike lay down on his bed. He didn't feel sleepy at all, suddenly, just empty. He stared at the angle of the dormered roof. He was conscious of a low hum of voices in conversation from downstairs. Through the open window came the click of goats' hooves as they played in their pen.

Then a dog barked. Mike dragged his mind to the sound with effort. To his complete surprise, the room was half dark. He had slept the afternoon completely away. Bucky's steady barking could only mean that a stranger was near the house. A knock at the door confirmed Mike's guess.

Still half asleep, Mike raced for the door. Mr. Orr stood in the vague-colored light of sundown, smiling at him.

"How's the responsible boy?" he asked cordially, taking Mike's hand enthusiastically in his own.

"I'm sorry," Mike said, shaking his head. "I was asleep. I'm fine and so are the kids," he added hastily.

"I know, I know," Mr. Orr agreed delightedly. "Had a little visit with them through the fence."

They talked only a few moments. Mike told Mr. Orr how sorry he was that his mother and father were not there to meet him, too.

"We'll meet," Mr. Orr confirmed. "I'm hoping you'll help me out some on weekends through the winter."

Mike hesitated, thinking of his own plans to be in Wichita, but Mr. Orr went on unheeding.

"I've got to get these little beasts home before it's dark."

After they had loaded the dancing kids onto the back of his pickup truck, Mr. Orr pressed a check in Mike's hand. "I'll be around to take away the fence and stuff later in the week," he explained. "There's a little bonus there for you."

After he had gone, Mike looked at the check. The little bonus was an extra week's pay. Altogether, Mike had twenty-eight dollars. A shiver of excitement ran through him. Surely this was enough to take him back to Wichita. Wichita! Home! Mike was so happy that he felt like he would burst open.

Car lights flashed against the garage. Mike watched Dad and Mom get out of the car slowly. It seemed strange to have only Elsie climb from the back seat, her face plainly tear-streaked.

"Mike," she wailed, hurling herself against him, "Merrie's all gone. She's all gone away."

Dad grinned, but Mike could tell it hadn't been easy for them to see Merrie go. He couldn't leave them now. His fingers pressed the check in his pocket. Later, when they were used to Merrie's being away, it would be different.

It really would.

6

THE UN-MERRIE DIFFERENCE

"I can't get over it," Mom said at breakfast the Tuesday that school started. "I was all prepared for Elsie to spend another year at home, but the teacher insisted over the phone that she is old enough to start.

"Maybe they aren't crowded for space here as they were in Wichita."

"When Merrie comes home at Christmas, I'll help her study," Elsie said smugly.

"Ho," Mike snorted, "you don't learn to read that fast."

"I do," Elsie replied haughtily.

Mom's face was still creased with a frown. "But I'm not sure I want her to go," she protested to Dad.

"Oh, come on, honey," he replied smiling, "she'll be six in November. It wouldn't be fair to hold her back a year."

"I'll tell you what," Mike suggested soberly, "I'll stay home and keep you from being lonesome."

"That's not the point at all!" Mom flared instantly.

Mike and Dad laughed. "Of course not," Dad said soothingly.

Mike waited a moment before asking the question that had bothered him for about a week.

"Mom, can I just take Elsie and walk her to school this morning?"

"What do you mean?" Mom asked, confused.

"I mean, I don't see why you have to go. The school's just down the road . . . not too far away. . . ." Mike's voice trailed off.

"I don't mind going," Mom said comfortingly. "I need the exercise."

It was Dad who understood. "Actually, it would probably be better, honey, if you would let the kids go alone. Elsie's already enrolled so she doesn't need you. Mike might have to take a pretty tough kidding from the other kids if they thought his mother had come to school with him."

"For heavens sakes!" Mom's eyes widened with surprise. "I never would have thought of that."

Mike smiled his thanks at Dad.

Elsie swung her lunch box back and forth importantly and chattered at Mike every step of the half mile down the hill to school.

Those last few yards before they reached the school seemed like a mile to Mike. Children were already clustered in the schoolyard. The older group stopped their talk and stared as Mike and Elsie approached. Mike was dreading this first morning at the new school. He was suddenly conscious of everything about himself. He envied Elsie her bland assurance. She ran from him to a group of small children playing near the swings.

A pretty girl with thick, dark curls tumbling down on to her collar was jumping a rope held by two others.

"Can I have a turn, too?" Elsie asked, without a moment's shyness.

"You have to turn the rope first," the dark-haired girl explained. Elsie set her lunch box down and took the rope. Mike shrugged. Maybe it was natural for everything to be twice as hard at eleven as it was at five going on six.

He stood uncertainly for only a minute before a tall boy broke from the group and sauntered towards him slowly. Mike immediately recognized him. He seemed taller now than he had seemed that day at Orr's End. He was slender and walked lightly as a good basketball player does. Even the shortness of his hair failed to conceal its curliness. He was smiling at Mike, but it was the coldest smile Mike could ever remember. Still, Mike was not prepared for his question.

The boy's voice was pitched low, but carried easily to the rest of the group.

"How is your Mommy today?" the boy asked, tenderly sarcastic.

Mike froze. What should he do? He didn't know a single one of the kids. If he started a fight right off, he had no way of knowing how they would react. Maybe he could play it straight, in the hope that behind one of those unknown faces might be at least one potential friend — for the little time that he would be here to need a friend.

"She's great," Mike replied slowly, then added, almost as insolently, "and how's yours?"

Mike was not in the least prepared for what happened. The boy stared at him, his face began to redden. Then suddenly, he struck Mike, not wildly at all, but purposefully. The blow caught Mike's face right on the angle of the chin, sending a sharp shaft of pain driving up through his head. He threw his arm up in defense against the rain of blows that followed. Instantly, they were surrounded, and the boy was pulled from him. A thick, pulsing pain persisted in Mike's jaw and up into his eye. Mike stared angrily at the group that held the dark-haired boy who was still straining and protesting to be released.

It took all Mike's courage to turn his back on the group and walk away. It was just sheer good luck that the first bell sounded as he neared the building. He didn't really have a place to go, he only knew that he could not stand there any longer watching the other boy's reasonless hatred being held from him by the other fellows.

He was just inside the schoolhouse door, looking around, when he felt a sudden touch on his elbow. A small, slender boy with a shock of sun-paled hair above round, dark-rimmed glasses, spoke quickly to him. "Don't pay any attention to Brad. He's kind of hot-

headed."

"You can say that," Mike replied, grinning painfully at him. "But thanks, anyhow."

It was one swell beginning, that's what, Mike brooded, as he followed the teacher's instructions, finding a seat and filling out a form for the files. He could feel the other kids' eyes on him and, in spite of himself, was acutely self-conscious.

There were four grades in the one room Mike learned as the morning progressed. Although there were only about thirty children in the room, they comprised all the fifth, sixth, seventh, and eighth grades in the district. He was to learn that Elsie, in the other room across the hall, was in a class of about the same size that included the first four grades.

He was one of eight sixth graders. Mike listened carefully as names were called. The dark-haired boy's name was Brad Mitchell. Mitchell surely seemed to be a very common name here. There was a set of Mitchell twins in the fifth grade, a girl and a boy named Peggy and Pat.

The morning went well enough. Books were issued and assignments made. Mike found himself increasingly more uncomfortable as the hours passed. His head ached and his jaw hurt every time he tried to answer the teacher. Yawning was out of the question! It hurt too much. He must have bitten his tongue when Brad's fist hit his jaw because he had the faintly salty taste of blood in his mouth. He dreaded lunch time when he would have to face the kids again. He wanted to be home more than anything in the world.

It was nearly noon when the teacher looked over at him strangely and asked, "Michael, are you feeling all right?"

"Why, yes, ma'am," Mike replied quickly.

"Your face looks swollen," she said thoughtfully, leaving the desk to walk towards him. Mike had liked her right off. She was older than Mom and built a little thickly without looking fat. She had a quiet, patient expression that made Mike comfortable right away.

Now she stood by his desk and peered intently at his face. "That eye is ripening like a cherry," she said lightly. "What do you suppose is causing that?"

"I can't say, ma'am," Mike countered quietly.

She looked at him, tapping her pencil against his desk. "You couldn't have hit it against anything without noticing it?"

Mike had to smile. She was certainly making it easy

for him. "I hardly think so," Mike replied.

"Maybe it's a bad tooth. Do you feel like going home?"

Mike hesitated only a minute. Going home would be wonderful. But how would he explain it to Mom? Then later, Elsie would have the unfamiliar walk home by herself. "Thank you. I'm fine," he said after a moment.

"Stop by my desk at noon if you want an aspirin or something," she suggested, and went back to the front of the class.

Mike could almost feel the class relax about him as their talk ended. It made him half angry. Did they think he was going to jump up like a kid and tattle on Brad Mitchell? He kept his glance down to keep from catching their eyes.

At noontime, the Mitchells, all three of them, Brad and the twins, went home for lunch. The other sixth graders took their lunches out to a patch of grass near the front of the school. The small, straw-haired boy, whose name was Tighe Williams, called to him. "Bring your lunch over here, Mike."

Mike sat by him and opened his lunch bag. He felt that his being there made them all self-conscious. Tighe saved the day by firing a series of questions at him. Mike explained that he was from Wichita and where his dad worked in town and where they lived.

"Hey, then you're the one who kept Mr. Orr's goats," a boy exclaimed.

"That's right," Mike replied. "How did you know?"

"I help Dad at the lumberyard summers," the boy explained. "I loaded the fencing and stuff for your yard."

"Brad wanted that job," someone commented.

"Oh, Brad wants every job," Susan said. "He wants jobs — but he never wants to work."

"He worked this summer all right," Tighe put in. "He helped his Dad put a new room on the house for the housekeeper. We added a porch at our place and believe me, that's work!"

"Did they get through?" Susan asked.

"No," Tighe replied. "Brad's dad told him that they had to finish it by basketball season or Brad couldn't have practice time. They'll make it easy, I think."

"I hope so," somebody said. "We sure need Brad on our team."

The talk went on to baseball, and there was a lively discussion of which boys from their school would be able to letter at the consolidated high school. Before Mike realized it, his lunch sack was empty and the time all gone. The bell rang while they were arguing over when the first skiing snow would cover the slopes.

While they were gathering their garbage up, the quiet, fair girl named Susan asked Mike quietly, "What did you say that set Brad off? We didn't hear it."

"He asked me how my mother was, so I told him she was great and asked him how his was."

Glances of quick understanding and nods of comprehension went about the group. When no one volunteered an explanation, Mike remarked, "I still don't see what I said wrong."

"You wouldn't," Susan said gently, "being a stranger. You see, Brad's mother died of polio about a year ago, and he's still pretty upset."

At Mike's look of dismayed regret, she went on hastily. "You couldn't possibly have known," she assured him. "Just bad luck, I guess."

When the long afternoon was finally over, Mike and Elsie walked home together.

Mike didn't really listen to Elsie's stream of chatter. His own thoughts were on the strange day. Maybe it was the newness of the combined classes, maybe it was the growing pain in the left side of his head that gave the whole day a sense of unreality. Whatever had caused it, he felt as if there were an invisible wall that shut him off from the others. He knew, just knew, in his heart that he couldn't ever, not in a million years, fit in with them and really belong, like Brad Mitchell did, or Tighe, or Susan.

Staying at school to avoid explanations at home turned out to be a silly idea.

Elsie kept Mom so busy that she didn't really take a square look at him, but Dad noticed his bruised face right away.

"Wow," Dad said in amazement. "Who hung one on you?"

"What do you mean?" Mike hedged.

"Listen to you," Dad laughed. He held Mike's chin lightly and pulled him in under the light. "You have a beautiful black eye coming there."

"Whatever are you talking about?" Mom asked, coming over to peer intently at Mike. She exploded into excited words. "Why, Mike, why, honey! What happened? Who did that?"

Dad stopped her spluttering with an upraised hand. "This won't be the last he'll get," he told her calmly. "What's the story, son?"

"Tansey's brother hit him in the face," Elsie said calmly. "Let's eat."

"Tansey?" Mom asked.

"She's my friend," Elsie explained proudly. "Her name's Tansey Mitchell, and they have a brother or sister for every day of the week at their house. Her brother hit my brother in the face."

"You want to tell us about it, son?" Dad asked quietly.

"I just answered him wrong," Mike said, hoping they would let it end there. Mom wouldn't have, except for Dad's expression.

"It's Mike's business," he told her. "If he wants our help, he knows he can come for it. Right, son?"

Mike nodded gratefully.

That night, Mike stared at the stars through the window in his room. He was acutely conscious of how far away Merrie was tonight. He could have told Merrie about the day. She would have talked to him and the whole thing would have been easier to figure out. Merrie was good at that. But Merrie was gone.

Mike got his money out and counted his twenty-eight dollars again before he finally went to bed and to sleep.

Tighe was the bright spot in the following weeks. He was an odd little fellow. He was an A student at school without apparently spending much energy on lessons. Although he was twelve, Tighe was not a whole lot taller than the fifth graders, and he had no coordination for sports at all.

The strange thing about him was that he didn't seem to care. He read through big stacks of books that he chose from the bookmobile that came to the school every other week, pursued his wide range of hobbies relentlessly, and gave a complete admiring enthusiasm to the athletic skill and hobbies of everyone else.

The first snow to cover the ground fell early the second week of October. Some had melted by noon, but the mountains were crowned with deepening shafts of white. It was a real snow.

The whole school bubbled with excitement.

"Only another month and the slopes will be ready," Susan explained happily to Mike at lunch, over a bowl of steaming soup that she had carried in her thermos. "Isn't that marvelous?"

"I've never skied," Mike admitted.

"He's a demon at jacks, though," Brad commented

dryly from beyond them.

Mike flushed. The steady harassment that Brad carried on was a needling irritation.

"This is the year I really learn!" Tighe said confidently.

A roar of laughter went up around the group. "Oh no, not again," someone groaned.

"So I'm a tanglefoot," Tighe shrugged. "I try."

"Tighe's the only person in Colorado who skis with his legs braided," Susan explained with a giggle. "Every season we spend half our time unwrapping him out of a drift. Then off he goes to the same trick again."

"I would do the same thing, I bet." Mike laughed.

"What do you mean 'would'? You will try, won't you?" Tighe asked quickly.

"If I'm here," Mike said without thinking.

"You aren't thinking of moving away or something, are you?" Susan asked.

"Not really," Mike corrected himself quickly. "Only, I'd sure like to go back to Wichita."

"I'd sure like that, too," Brad said caustically. "I'd like that fine."

"Oh, come off it, Brad," Tighe said, half disgustedly.

Every week now brought two- or three-inch snows during the nights. Dad left for work before daylight and returned after night had fallen. Mike shoveled away at the walks and driveway. Usually he went down the road to give their old neighbor, Mr. Pederson, a hand with his snow. The snow drifted like waves over the neat rows of the gooseberry garden.

By Halloween week, the drifts were six and seven feet high where the snow from the road had been plowed back. The mountain was a white blanket, patterned with great loops of pleasure etched by the sleds and skis of the town children.

"Looks more like Christmas than Halloween," Dad commented at dinner. "Remember how warm it was this time last year in Wichita?"

"Will I have to go back there when Mike goes?" Elsie asked, suddenly looking up from her plate.

"What makes you think Mike's going?" Mom asked, surprised.

"That what Tansey's brother said," Elsie replied defensively. "And he says it can't be too soon for him!"

Although Mike didn't look up, he could feel his father's searching eyes on him. "What about that, son?"

Dad asked quietly.

Mike was struggling for a way to answer Dad. "I've always liked Wichita," Mike said finally, without meeting his father's eye.

"Mike's going to take me trick or treating," Elsie interrupted. "And I going to be a Eskimo."

"An Eskimo," Mom corrected.

"You still feel that way, son?" Dad asked, sounding almost puzzled.

Mike could feel Dad waiting for his answer. As Mom and Elsie chattered on, Mike kept his eyes on his plate. He had thought it through. He had earned the money, then he had waited for his parents to get used to Merrie being gone. He had waited and tried to be a part of this place and these people. Hadn't he given it a fair chance?

Suddenly, the plates were being cleared for dessert. Mike got up to help Mom. He felt Dad's eyes, hurt and puzzled, still on him as he turned away.

7

THE NIGHT OF THE TORCHES

The night of Halloween was like Christmas. A nearly full moon cast long, blue shadows across the banked snow. Little scudding wisps of darker clouds crossed and recrossed the moon's face.

Elsie was unbearably excited. Bundled to the ears, with her long hair caught up into the fur-trimmed parka, she looked like an Eskimo elf behind her little half-face mask. In her wooly mittens, she clutched a trick-or-treat bag that she had decorated at school.

Mike bundled up warmly, too. If Elsie was to visit more than one house, he would have a three or four mile

pull along the snowy road with Elsie on the sled.

Mom looked a little unhappily at the big wooden bowl of caramel apples on sticks. "I'll just feel terrible if nobody comes here," she told Mike. "That's half the fun."

"I'll come," Elsie assured her, eyeing the candied apples hungrily.

Mike had a feeling that their neighbors, the Pedersons, went to bed early, so he pulled Elsie across the road to the gooseberry house first. When Mr. Pederson opened the door and saw Elsie standing little better than knee-high in the snow with her orange sack, he laughed heartily. "Come in, come in, little Eskimo." He peered into the darkness where Mike waited. "Don't you have a big friend with you?"

When Elsie nodded yes, Mr. Pederson called for Mike to come, too.

As much time as he had spent with Mr. Pederson, Mike had never met his wife before. She was a small, smiling woman with gray hair caught tightly in a high bun behind her head. Her small spectacles were as round as little half dollars of glass. The Pedersons were deliriously happy to see them. Instead of a treat, she had set a small table by the blazing fire. On it was a pitcher of milk and squares of hot gingerbread topped with whipped cream.

"Ooh, does that look good!" Elsie said, hastily shedding her mittens and parka.

"We were hoping you'd be sure and stop here," Mrs. Pederson said, bustling about and getting Elsie into a small chair. "We don't get many children up on our part of the hill. Now Mr. Orr has a regular party at his place, so the kids always go that way."

The gingerbread was delicious. Mike ate a second piece quite as much to please her as for how good it tasted.

When they had finished and thanked their neighbors again, Mike got Elsie set on the sled. The old couple stood in the door watching.

"You youngsters come back often, now," Mrs. Pederson urged. "You can't know how much it means watching you go by to school and having you folks close."

The warmth of that fire seemed to stay with them. Elsie squealed with delight as Mike jogged along almost at a run to the next group of houses. She rang three more doorbells before Mike insisted that they start back.

They met only two other groups of youngsters on

their side of the hill, but Mike was surprised to see a lot of car traffic going towards Goldstream. When they drew near enough to see their own house, Elsie commented, "Mommy got her wish."

"What do you mean?" Mike asked.

"Two cars just stopped at our house. I saw them," Elsie replied.

Mike had been watching the track. Now he looked up the road. Sure enough, one car was just then pulling away from in front of their house.

"Maybe we better hurry if you're going to get one of those caramel apples," he warned.

Suddenly, he stopped. He had chanced to look past the house. Up the side of the mountain about where the plateau was, he had seen a light. He stared and waited.

"Come on, I'm getting cold," Elsie protested.

Mike walked on slowly and absently, still watching. The light came again. Over to the west, several yards beyond it, another light twinkled a quick blinking that came and went in almost a second. Then he saw another and another.

"Look at the lights on the hill," he said to Elsie. "Count them."

"What are they?" Elsie asked, half scared.

Mike shrugged.

"They're ghosts, I know it!" Elsie began to whimper. "Hurry Mike, hurry up home."

With Elsie still sniveling, Mike spun the sled up the drive and let her off at the back door.

He was standing staring up at the vagrant lights that crawled the slopes as Mom came out, shivering under a light sweater. She shut the door behind her as if to keep Elsie from hearing.

"Do you see that?" Mike asked her.

She nodded, looking a little sick.

Mike stared at her. "What's the matter, Mom?"

"There's a child lost on the mountain," she said quietly.

"You're kidding," Mike cried. "In that deep snow . . . and at night? Who is it?" he asked, shivering as much from the thought of the lost child as from the cold.

"Some men came. They were in such a hurry they didn't say any name. They came to borrow all our lanterns for the search. Dad went with the last group that came by."

A square of light fell on the snow. Elsie stood in the open door.

"Come on in, what's the matter?" she asked querulously into the darkness where Mike and Mom stood talking.

"Coming, darling," Mom said quickly, adding in a whisper to Mike, "don't say anything to Elsie. She's so easily upset."

Mike nodded. He hung up the sled thoughtfully before following her in.

The caramel apple was as good as it looked. Mike ate it slowly while he worked his math problems for the next day. From upstairs, he could hear Elsie's rapid chattering account of their trick-or-treating as Mom scrubbed her in the hot tub and slipped her, still talking, into bed.

Mom came downstairs slowly, not attempting to conceal her concern from Mike.

"Isn't it awful about that child, Mike?" she said. "What if it were our Elsie?"

"How in the world did it ever happen?" Mike asked. "The kids in school know the mountains too well to take chances in the snow and dark."

Mom shrugged. "It surprised me, too. But it seems that it is a sort of community tradition for Mr. Orr to have a great big party every Halloween. He has games and prizes and lots of good things to eat. The town children all go to Orr's End sometime during the evening. A group of youngsters had left and been gone a while and then came back to ask if the missing child were still there. They checked the house and grounds.

"That was when they found the gate of the goat pen open and the goats gone. The snow was all trampled about as if the child had tried to get them back in — just like Elsie, last summer. The trail led to the woods before they lost it. The woods are full of hunter's footprints and the snow is never very deep under the tall trees this early."

Mike shook his head. The woods had such a sameness. He remembered his own great fear of being lost in them.

"I sure wish you'd let me go help search, Mom," he pleaded. "It's not that awfully cold tonight, and the goats know my voice."

Mom shook her head. "The townspeople surely know that hill as well as anyone."

Mom was standing by the window, outside the round flood of light from the old-fashioned lamp that hung low over the dining table.

"Did I tell you that the men who came for the lanterns said that two of the goats came back an hour later?" Mom said suddenly.

"Which two?" Mike asked.

"They didn't say." Mom sighed. "There was an odd thing. Nobody seemed to understand this. It isn't thawing anywhere, yet the two goats had been in water. Their coats were frozen solid."

Mike leaped to his feet. "That does it, Mom. You have to let me go. I know where they are!"

Mom stared at him. "How can you be sure?"

Mike threw his notebook and books together. "I tell you, Mom, I know. Nobody . . . none of the kids at school will believe me when I tell them about the cave with the pool where I found the kids last summer. They swear that there's no opening for that underground river through the mountain since the mines were closed down and the shafts sealed. But I know. And that's where they are. I'm sure!"

He was pulling his boots on swiftly. Mom didn't argue any more. "Let me call somebody to get you," she said. "It's so far in the cold."

Mike shook his head. "I can run and keep warm. And I've got to hurry because only I can find the cave that nobody else believes in."

"I hope you're right. Please be careful," Mom called after him as he started down the road towards town at a fast-paced trot.

"I will be," Mike called over his shoulder. But already a small wiggle of doubt was starting in his mind. He was right about the cave, but would he be able to find it from the Orr's End side of the hill, with snow and winter changing the familiar face of the mountain?

8

AND HOW IT ENDED

Mike's hours of baseball practice paid off as he jogged down the icy road into town. There was something unbelievably weird about this night. He trotted along the main street of Goldstream, past stores whose windows were still lit with orange-and-black jack-o-lanterns and ghostly lights. The big pumpkin in the drugstore window cast an eerie orange light on the banked snow.

Mike's wind almost gave out on the steep hill that rose towards Orr's End. He could see the house blazing with lights from quite a distance. The last few hundred yards of the road were blocked with parked cars and trucks.

Mike leaped over the stone wall and went directly to the great front door. He had barely released the knocker when a strange woman opened the door. She looked at Mike questioningly.

"I have to see Mr. Orr," Mike said swiftly. "Tell him . . ." he knew his name would not help much, "tell him it's the boy from Jensen's Place."

She nodded and motioned for him to follow her.

Mr. Orr was talking on the phone. He was speaking swiftly and loudly. Mike knew it must be either a long distance call or country party line, for he was almost yelling. He had to repeat his message several times before the person on the other end understood. He was telling them about the lost child and asking them to send a search party north and west of Orr's End.

He sighed when he laid the phone down. Even with his yelling silenced, the house was still a hubbub. In the room beyond, several women were working and steadily talking, making sandwiches and brewing pots of coffee. The room was filled with the steam from wet clothing and boots drying on folded newspapers. A couple of men were engrossed in a roughly drawn map all criss-crossed with lines.

"Hi," Mr. Orr said warmly. "Did you come to help?"

He nodded with approval that glowed inside Mike.

"Listen, Mr. Orr. . . ." Mike began to tumble out what he knew about the cave.

When he first began to talk, Mr. Orr had interrupted. "We know every inch of these hills, son," but as Mike talked on, the older man leaned forward and cocked his head, listening intensely. Suddenly, he interrupted.

"Tell me. Was there a rock pile around?"

Mike nodded. "All about the opening there are rocks. Some were covered with brush, but those at the mouth were clean and quite new looking. There is such a heavy growth of trees about the place that you have to look very hard to find it."

"A pool, and an opening into the hill?" Mr. Orr insisted, as if it were very very important for Mike to have it exactly right.

"Beyond this one deep pool, the river, or whatever it is, runs through a big cave back into the mountains. It has shelves along the side, like walkways or something," Mike repeated. "The goats were sleeping on that ledge the day Bucky chased them away."

Someone called from the door, but Mr. Orr held his hand up for silence and stared at Mike thoughtfully.

"We know that underground river in the mountain

comes from a spring somewhere. If that spring and its pool had been hidden by rocks all these years and then the rocks shifted free, as they do, for no reason that we ever know," he went on hesitatingly, "then an opening would be formed into the mountain. Can you lead me there?"

"I think so," Mike said slowly, the same numb fear beginning again. "I have never gone to it from this side of the mountain before, and there is snow."

"But you are willing to try?"

"Of course," Mike said surprised. "That's why I came, sir."

Mr. Orr rose, talking rapidly now. "Lanterns. Are you warm enough?"

Mike nodded and followed Mr. Orr into the adjoining room. Within seconds, it seemed to Mike, Mr. Orr was bundled in warm clothes, and they both were handed lanterns. The women working in the kitchen as well as the men warming up for their next trip out stared curiously at them as they passed through.

"This is the boy from Jensen's Place," he told them. "He says there's a cave opening into the underground river. We're going there to look."

They left the house by the back door. Only a few

yards farther on, two figures crossed the yard and came toward them.

"Mitch," Mr. Orr called. Mike only then recognized the smaller of the two figures. It was Brad Mitchell.

"This is the boy from Jensen's Place," Mr. Orr began. "He thinks he knows a place. . . ."

Brad broke in angrily. "He doesn't know anything, Dad."

The man cautioned the boy to silence. Mike liked Mr. Mitchell's looks. With a heavy parka over his bulky clothes, he seemed to be an amazingly big man. Dark hair fell on his forehead and his open face was tense with concern.

"We'll try anything," the man said swiftly, searching Mike with his eyes.

Brad stood sullenly. "Come or stay?" his father asked tersely.

"Come," Brad muttered, his tone implying the foolishness of the journey.

The three men followed Mike's hesitant progress up the slope. They talked very little. "We've been all over this hill a dozen times," Brad said.

"Hush or go back," his father answered.

"Which goats came back, Mr. Orr?" Mike asked.

"Rick and Tawny," Mr. Orr replied. "It's Tick who's gone." Mike heard Brad repeat "Goats" in a scathing undertone.

Mike tried to ignore Brad's irritating attitude. He had to concentrate on his distances. He had measured it the way Dad had taught him, by counting strides to gauge feet and yards.

The trouble was that all the clearings looked the same covered by ice.

Mike was really cold now. He had sweated during his run from home to Orr's End. Because of his damp clothes, the rising wind and the outside air were beginning to chill him. His face was frozen into a block of scarlet pain and his eyes and lips smarted from the needles of cold.

And he was afraid, increasingly afraid for the lost child . . . whoever it was . . . having seen the desperate organization of the search being carried on from Orr's End. He was apprehensive, too, of the insolent ridicule that failure would be sure to earn from Brad.

They broke through a ring of trees. Mike stopped. This should be it. It was a clearing all right, but how could he be sure? The drifts filled half of it. If, he thought suddenly, if the remains of his wooden trail marker were under that drift, then he would know for sure. There were tracks everywhere. A dust of fine snow had begun to fall making them indistinct.

Mike went swiftly to the center of the clearing. Without explanation, he began to kick at the low drifts. They watched him in a stunned silence. Great clouds of snow swirled up and sparkled in the lights from their lanterns. Suddenly a stick flew. Mike kneeled and shouted exultantly. Bending, he pulled out another and another and another from the drifts and threw them happily.

"This is it," he cried. "Quick, which way is north?"

Mr. Mitchell pointed and Mike struck off to the northeast into the trees. They followed him closely and silently. Only a few feet beyond the clearing, he separated the wall of frozen shrub, and they saw the pool. The ice that had been broken in jagged points was now refrozen into a thick, shivery slush.

With the lantern in his hand, Mike threw himself down by the pool and angled a light into the dark cavern beyond the pool.

The light in the cave brought a million twinkling mica-like reflections from the roof and the sides of the hollowed-out rock.

Suddenly, from the shelf, below the yellow beam of the lantern, came a hesitant cry. "Baaa?" Tick asked gently, as if to inquire if this disturbance were really necessary.

Mike shifted the light beam. What appeared to be a small witch was curled on the ledge beside Tick. The goat did not bother to get up but stared at them, chewing thoughtfully. His round stomach served as a warm pillow for the sleeping child. A fervent "Thank God" sounded behind Mike.

Mr. Orr was slapping his mittens together excitedly.

"How can we get her out?" Mr. Mitchell asked. "If she stirs, she'll fall off into the water, and that opening is too small for a man."

Mike was not waiting. He let himself down into the pool, feeling with his boot for the shallow side. The sound of the crunching ice made the child stir. Mike moved swiftly, heedless of the icy water rising nearly to his waist. He crawled through the opening and gently took the curled up child from the ledge into his arms. She stirred and stared up at him.

"Why, Tansey," he cried in amazement.

"Who did you think it was?" Mr. Orr queried from outside. Mike carefully felt for his footing, weaving a

little under the child's weight.

As soon as Mike could stand up in the pool, Mr. Mitchell seized the child and held her against him.

As Mike stepped from the water, Tick followed him out. She bleated cordially at them and rubbed her little knobby head against Mr. Orr's trousers.

Tansey wakened slowly, yawned widely, and smiled at her father through half-closed eyes. "She's warm as a bug," Mr. Mitchell said in amazement.

Suddenly Tansey's eyes flew wide. She looked scared. "Daddy," she cried, "I let Mr. Orr's goats out. I didn't mean to at all. But Brad had said so much about them, I wanted to see them close, and make friends with them like Elsie did. But the minute I got the gate open, they pushed me over and ran away."

Mr. Mitchell sighed, "Honestly, Brad. All that talk about the goats. As if you didn't have enough to do to help me." Brad didn't reply. He looked down at his feet as if reluctant to meet anyone's eyes.

"They're all right now," Mr. Orr said soothingly. "But, Tansey, you shouldn't have gone off into the woods with them."

"I didn't 'tend to," she said drowsily. "They just kept running and I kept trying to bring them back."

"How did you get in there without falling into the water?" her father asked.

"I just oonched along that edge," Tansey said matter-of-factly. "The goat jumped in, but it looked too cold to me."

Mike watched her. Like Mom, he kept thinking of Elsie, even more now that he realized that the lost child was Elsie's little friend that she talked of so constantly . . . and Brad's sister.

Tansey was right about the water being cold. Mike's clothing was completely soaked. The chill was driving to his bones like a knife. In spite of himself, his teeth began to chatter.

"Hey, hey," Mr. Orr said, "we've got to get this boy some dry clothes."

He clapped Mike on the shoulder. "You're all right, you are, boy," he said gruffly.

Mr. Mitchell looked at Mike. He struggled for words without success. He nodded and smiled at Mike. Mike nodded back. There weren't words. They didn't need them anyway Mike realized, almost with surprise.

Brad carried Tick, who looked about brightly from his arms all the way home. Tansey was still drowsy and nestled silently against her father.

Shouts of excited relief greeted their arrival. The signal gun was fired to notify the searchers that the child had been found.

While Mike was stripping off his saturated clothes, he could hear the men coming in the back door. He heard their excited questions and the rumbles of the story being told again and again. Mike's dad was among the late arrivals. He came in while Mike was getting warm clothes on and wrapped a warm blanket around Mike's shoulder. He stood and looked at Mike a long moment, and then scrubbed Mike's head the way Merrie always did, his knuckles hard against Mike's scalp.

"Good boy," he said quietly. It was enough.

Mr. Orr's clothes were much too big for Mike, but at least they were warm and dry. Mike was reluctant to re-enter the rooms where the exultant searchers were celebrating the success over huge platters of sandwiches and strong coffee that filled the air with a rich, acrid smell. For one thing, he felt funny. He had a dull pounding in the back of his head, and he felt hot all over.

"Come on, son," Dad urged. "I need to get my wet boots off."

"You go on, Dad," Mike said. "I'll be right along."

After Dad left, certain that Mike would immediately follow, Mike sat down on the edge of the bed. He hoped nobody would come in for a minute. He felt almost sick at his stomach now. He shook his head to clear it. His face hurt where his cheeks had gotten so cold.

He heard the voice at the door asking. "Where is he? Where is the boy from Jensen's Place?" As the door opened, Mike sneezed loudly as if in answer. The friendliest burst of laughter Mike had ever heard filled the room.

He drank a steaming mug of hot cocoa and nodded and tried to keep smiling as the townspeople milled about and congratulated him. His eyes were heavy with sleep once he finished the hot drink, and he was completely grateful when his Dad insisted that he bundle up and go back home so Mom could see for herself that he was all right.

9

THE SIX-FOOT BUS TICKET

Later, Mike could hardly remember getting home at all. He must have been half asleep from fatigue and cold and the sudden relief of finding Tansey safe.

He wakened a little before dawn the next day, with a sharp chill pain in his side. He twisted about, and when it wouldn't go away, he finally called to Mom.

The doctor who came was a heavy-set, gray man. At least he seemed gray to Mike in that dawn light. His suit was of a pepper-and-salt color and his beard and hair matched it. Only his eyes were colorful, bright blue and dancing.

He kidded Mike while he examined him. "Around here we don't go in much for this polar bear swimming," he told Mike. "Maybe you won't either after last night."

Mike could hear him still talking to Mom and Dad in the hall as he drifted off to sleep.

When he finally wakened again, Mike heard an easy, familiar rhythm that he could not at first identify. It was a back-and-forth rhythm with a little creaking somewhere in the middle. Someone in the room was humming an aimless little tune that didn't sound like a song at all, more like a small bee bumbling its content.

When he opened his eyes, he saw the familiar dormers of his room angling above him. Great shafts of icicles laced his window, catching the sunlight and breaking it like a prism against the inside wall.

The rhythm stopped. He looked over and saw little Mrs. Pederson rise from the rocker and fold her knitting.

"Well, and it's about time." She smiled. She laid a small, blue-veined hand on his coverlet briefly. Then she walked to the door and called down the stairs. "The sleepy head is awake."

Mike heard Mom's steps coming swiftly up the stairs. She entered like a whirlwind. After staring at him wordlessly a moment, she kissed him hard, missing his mouth completely. Mrs. Pederson slipped out as Mom entered.

"Boy, I feel like I've been asleep forever," Mike told Mom as she pulled up the little rocker that the neighbor had been using.

"It seemed almost that long to us, too," Mom said brightly. "You *have* been sick. You still are," she added hastily.

"That's silly," he said slowly, realizing that talking didn't come too easily. It hurt his chest when he drew a deep breath. The dull pounding in the back of his head had started again now that he had opened his eyes.

"Silly or no," Mom said tartly, "you must have gotten thoroughly chilled on the way to Orr's that night. The dip in the pool and the walk back finished you off."

"It was cold all right. But, gosh, Mom, who ever passed out from a cold?"

"Not very many," she admitted, "but pneumonia is a little more than that."

"Oh, nuts," Mike said emphatically. "How can a guy catch pneumonia and not know it?"

"Maybe you had your mind on other things," she smiled.

"Where's Elsie? Does she know about Tansey yet?"

Mom nodded. "It was all over school the next day.

Elsie is proud as punch of you."

Mike sat up or tried to, and immediately lay back down. "All over school *the next day?*"

"Today is the third of November, in case you've lost track," she grinned. "You missed a couple in there. High fever and the drugs and all." She grinned. "You're fine now, though. The doctor says a couple of weeks."

"Couple of weeks?" Mike's voice squeaked unexpectedly. "But what about school?"

"Arrangements are all made," she said lightly. "Don't worry about it now. Hungry?"

He saw Mrs. Pederson standing in the door smiling at them. "What I'd really like is a piece of gingerbread with whipped cream," he said.

She laughed and shook her head. "Listen to that flatterer."

"That makes today Friday, doesn't it?" he asked Mom as she took the tray of soup and crackers from Mrs. Pederson.

"That's right. Elsie is due home any time."

As Mrs. Pederson went downstairs, Mom said, "She came over to offer her help for you. The phone has rung steadily these days and people are always stopping by to ask. I really don't know how we could have gotten along without her. Mrs. Pederson's a darling, isn't she? Almost," she added wistfully, "like having Grandma around.

"She's really won Dad's heart, too. She thinks she can't let him run out of gooseberry pie, and you know how well that suits him."

The warm soup made Mike drowsy. He didn't hear Mom leave or even hear Elsie come from school. When he wakened again, it was to his Dad's voice asking gently, "Hey, son, do you feel like having company?"

Mike smiled. "Sure, Dad. Gee, how are you?"

"Oh, I'm fine," Dad laughed. "Let me tell you all about my health."

"Okay," Mike laughed. "I'm better, thanks."

"No kidding, son, there are a couple of fellows . . . three in fact, who have been waiting downstairs to see you. Do you feel up to a visit?"

"Sure, Dad." Mike looked the question, but Dad didn't answer. He only went to the top of the stairs and called down. "The sleeping beauty is awake."

Suddenly, it seemed that the room was filled with men. Mr. Mitchell, even with his parka off, was a big, broad man, and his smile was warm and wide enough to fill any room. His grasp on Mike's hand was almost painful.

"There's no way to thank you, really," he told Mike. "I'm just going to depend on you to understand."

Mike nodded his head. "It was just that I happened to know that cave . . . and Tick," he replied.

"Okay, so you knew about the cave. But from what I've heard, you've no good basis for risking even a sniffle for the Mitchell clan."

Mike felt sorry for Brad standing uneasily in the back of the room listening to his father's words.

"Gosh, Mr. Mitchell," Mike said defensively, "Brad and I just got off to a bad start." It was true. It still pained Mike to remember what a bad accident it had been for him to answer Brad back with the only words that could have cut that deeply.

"Anyway, that's all over," Mike added, hoping he was right.

"Yeah," Brad said suddenly. "It'll be different now, Mike."

"That's the first time you've ever called me by name, Brad," Mike said surprised.

" 'That boy from Jensen's Place' didn't sound right after Halloween," Mr. Mitchell said quietly.

"Is Tansey really all right?" Mike asked.

"Ha!" Brad replied, "meaner than ever. You'd think she had saved your life the way she tells it."

"She and Elsie are two of a kind, I guess." Mike laughed.

"My sympathy," Brad replied.

There was a restless movement at the back of the room. Someone was standing there by Dad. Mike pulled up on his elbows.

"Tighe," he said with happy surprise.

"Hi," Tighe replied almost shyly. "I brought you something."

"Gee, thanks," Mike said, taking the package. It was a book. He could tell through the wrapping. As the paper fell away, a burst of laughter echoed about the room.

"I read it first," Tighe said hastily. "It makes real good sense." He read the title aloud, "*Slalom Technique.*" The little bedside lamp caught his glasses, making an owl-bright reflection.

"Thanks, Tighe, really thanks," Mike said. After a minute he added honestly, "What's a slalom?" He stumbled on the word a little and laughter filled the room again.

"It's the kind of skiing you'll probably like best," Brad put in. "The slopes will be good just about when you get ready to go out. Mike's never skied, Dad," Brad added to his father. "Don't you think we could teach him?"

"We'd sure have fun trying." Mr. Mitchell grinned at the prospect. "Some learn quicker than others," he added, with a look at Tighe.

Tighe laughed. "I'm the kind of student you never lose by graduation," he said with satisfaction.

After they all left, Dad sat by Mike for a long time in the half-dark room.

Dad finally got up to leave, stopped at the door, and came back.

"They wanted to reward you for what you did," Dad said, "but I told them you'd rather not be paid. I was right, wasn't I?"

"Of course you were," Mike replied quickly.

"Anyway, you still must have most of your kid-sitting money," Dad said.

Mike nodded.

"Saving it?" Dad asked.

Mike nodded again.

"Can I ask for what?" his dad asked quietly.

Mike couldn't think of a way to say it. Finally he said, "Maybe you can guess, Dad."

"Something like a bus ticket to Wichita?" Dad asked gently.

Mike nodded again, and the room was quiet.

"Dad," Mike said finally. "I still want to use the money, but the bus ticket is a different kind now."

Dad looked at him, waiting.

"What I have in mind is a bus ticket about six feet long, to run up and down the mountain on."

Dad cocked his head and then laughed. "A six-foot long bus ticket. Do some people call them skis?"

Mike nodded agreement.

"I want you to be sure, Mike," Dad said soberly. "You won't always be the hero of the hour here. You may be as good a skier as your friend, Tighe. Things don't unruffle all at once, you know."

"I know, Dad," Mike agreed slowly. "But whenever you can't run away home without leaving something you'll miss, it's time to stay."

Dad pushed his shoulder gently. "Right, Mike. You

best get to sleep. There's many a spill between you and the slaloms."

As he started to shut the door behind him, he stuck his head back in and said, "Six-foot bus ticket, indeed."

And they both laughed.

Born in Kansas, Mary Francis Shura has lived in Missouri and Nebraska and has recently moved to Atlanta, Georgia with her husband, Raymond Craig, and their four children including Baby Shay, a recent addition to the family.

She is, obviously, in an unusually good position to know the problems and eventual joys that beset a family when they must pull up their roots and move. RUNAWAY HOME is a sensitive portrayal of how one family, and particularly their eleven year old boy, Mike, make the adjustment when they must move from Kansas to Colorado, and how Mike finally finds that home is not so much a specific place as where your family and friends are.